Eyecatcher

Eyecatcher

MIKE KRECIALA

KINDREDSON PUBLISHING LIMITED

Published by
Kindredson Publishing Limited,
9 Bank Buildings, Llandeilo,
Dyfed, SA19 6BU.

ISBN 0–951299 8 1 6

*Printed in Wales by
Dynevor Printing Company,
Rawlings Road, Llandybie,
Dyfed, SA18 3YD.*

*This novel is a work of fiction.
Any resemblance to actual events or persons,
living or dead, is entirely coincidental.*

To my family
with love

FOREWORD

Venturing into the domain of the world wide renowned racing novelist Dick Francis is a bold step to take yet, in *Eyecatcher*, Mike Kreciala has come up with a story Dick would be proud to have hatched himself.

The mixture of horse racing, international business, the internal workings of the police force and a good range of characters, keeps the reader's interest right to the end.

When the author adds the teaser of allowing the reader to think he is ahead of the plot, an immediate reversal of strategy will make you kick yourself for falling into the trap.

Eyecatcher is an incredibly good racehorse in this fictional story although, on reflection, there is a great deal of fact in Mike's intriguing thriller.

You can almost smell the horses in this fast-moving novel with enough sex and humour to make you wonder if, after all, policemen are as human as horsey folk.

Richard Pitman

ACKNOWLEDGEMENTS

My thanks firstly to my colleagues in the Dyfed Powys police for their support and encouragement.

My gratitude for the assistance, guidance and information given to me by the following: Peter Hopkins, Debbie and Bryan Smart, Mike Hughes and Eric and Christine Carberry.

Thanks are also due to my friends in the veterinary profession, Bertie Ellis, Philip Michael and members of the Llandeilo practices, for the veterinary knowledge that they so readily gave to me.

I am indebted to Sue Beetlestone for preparing the manuscript, to Dynevor Printing Company for their care and diligence, and to Bernard and Paul Kindred for their patience and enthusiasm.

I acknowledge the help given to me by Wetherbys and I am very grateful to Richard Pitman for writing the foreword and his considerable advice and encouragement.

Above all no words can repay the debt I owe to my wife Liz, my parents and Nan for their loyalty and support which made the writing even more enjoyable.

CHAPTER ONE

Police constable Thomas Cord climbed the stairs to the flat in subdued excitement and expectation. The sight of Pamela's beautiful buttocks inches in front led him, step by step, like a ringed bull. They were so prominently out of proportion with the rest of her body that his eyes were drawn to them as if to an optician's wall chart.

Thomas was clean-cut, clean-shaven and always cared about his appearance. Now, worried about his hair style which had been flattened by his helmet all day, he tried to finger-comb it back into perfection as he followed behind her.

In public he had tried to avoid staring at her voluptuous bottom half, feeling that people were watching him and guessing what was going on in his mind. God! Now he couldn't keep his eyes off. This was the first time he'd been alone with her and only the second time they'd spoken to each other. He knew she worked in the hairdressers; he also knew she lived on the second floor above it. He'd made a point of finding out after noticing her in a bank queue but, after following her, he was too shy to go any further and now . . . Boy! How she moved! The rest of her was inviting enough, blonde hair with a peekaboo cut giving her that mixture of class and a come-to-bed look. She had a slim figure, with firm ample breasts and faultless legs, but he was transfixed on that main attraction, superb below her tiny waist. And yet, he thought, in her eyes this was probably her worst feature, the part she'd always wished she could change. He let the thought fade. This was no time to analyse.

But for the scar, Thomas could have been good looking. He'd always remained self-conscious about it, a cruel looking slash which followed a diagonal line for two-and-a-half inches down the left side of his face, from the eyebrow to the cheek bone, just touching the outside corner of his eye. The scar might have spoilt his looks, but it hadn't spoiled his chances. In fact, it seemed to attract the females.

Fellow police officers had named him 'Doorstop' for they, together with friends and those he loved, knew the mundane truth – how it had been caused by a school accident, someone slamming a glass door in his face. But others, too embarrassed to ask, he'd leave uninformed, allowing them in their imagination to link the scar to some brave conflict.

However, the one thing that did undoubtedly give him an unfair advantage was his eyes. To the envy of his sister, Thomas had his mother's eyes, Atlantic eyes, deep, soulful and blue, made all the more so by a hint of porcelain in the whites.

It was the scar that interested the women and the eyes which held them.

Women! – now, at thirty-four, he still couldn't say no to them.

Pamela invited him to the flat after dancing with

him the previous night and that, in itself, had been unexpected. He wasn't sure if she'd overheard the sexual comment he'd made to his colleague as they stood at the door of the disco, or if she had caught him staring but, as he turned to walk out, she ran up behind him and asked him for a dance. He didn't want to embarrass her with a refusal and, besides, this was the chance he'd wanted. But, in full police uniform, how could he . . . What the hell, he'd thought. He told his colleague Richard Speak, also on duty and in uniform, to wait for him. Standing 5ft 11″, Richard was an inch shorter than Thomas. He had a boy's twinkling eyes and a nose that dipped when he smiled. He wore the standard policeman's moustache, had the one girlfriend to whom he'd become engaged, and had no worries. Thomas took Pamela to the side of the dance floor, to the shadows where he hoped to be less conspicuous. Dancing while on duty, he felt uneasy and held her close, hoping to hide as best he could. But hiding was impossible and well he knew it. She put her head on his chest and he realised that his hands were resting on those beautiful buttocks.

"Listen," he said, "I must go after this dance or my police car will turn into a pumpkin."

"Are you married?" she asked, ignoring his words.

"Yes, I am, but don't tell my girlfriend! Can I see you again?" he whispered.

"Okay," she said. "Call 'round tomorrow, I live on top of . . ."

"I know where you live," he said, cutting her short.

"Well, I might sleep at my friend's tonight, so

don't bother ringing the bell until you see the milk's been taken in."

He had walked the beat the following day having doubled backed to a day shift starting at 10am. The milk, a white sentry, had remained on her doorstep throughout, protecting her from being disturbed. Was she teasing him? Watching from an upstairs window perhaps, or had she forgotten, or did she have someone else there? This thought made him jealous, but he dare not ring in case a stranger were to answer. That pint of milk had divided his day into eight equal tours of the town and at 6pm, it was still there, but now, at 6.30 he was off duty and, like the milk, he was being taken inside.

Thomas was frustrated from the torment of waiting, his jealousy building up from the lack of any explanation. Because of this she was in control, leading him up the stairs, expecting him to follow. They reached the top and she led him into her flat, through a kitchen and into a room which reflected her personality – totally feminine and yet strong in its originality. The decor was stylishly enriched with subtle lighting and art nouveau figures, without sacrificing that lived-in atmosphere – lived-in by a girl who was neat and clean. He looked at her and saw more than a pair of buttocks. At that moment he was in love, yet the feeling was short lived and was soon overtaken by lust – pure animal magnetism. That was what had brought him here and there was no point in denying it.

"You are married, aren't you?" she asked.

"Yes, but I'm not superstitious," he answered.

"Well," she said, "you can come here for a coffee,

as a friend now and again, but there's not going to be anything more than that – there's no point."

She put a record of The Pretenders on the stereo – a strong female voice but at a volume that didn't intrude. She left him briefly and went into the kitchen. He looked around the room and dared to pick up one of the figures. Surprisingly, it was genuine – a Preiss. He replaced it as Pamela returned, bringing him what she had described as his 'friendly coffee'. She sat on the floor, her back supported by the side of the low bed. With the bed as the only alternative place to sit and having been neutered by her last cutting remarks, he settled on the floor next to her. Thomas felt indecisive as he awkwardly put his arm around her, a virgin boy in the back seat of the pictures with a girl who obviously wasn't a virgin. Pamela had turned him from a positive policeman into a schoolboy on his first date, not knowing whether to slip his hand over her breast or not.

"How did you get that scar?" she asked.

"Glass, nothing much," he admitted, "a school accident."

She wasn't impressed.

He turned to kiss her, but she suddenly got up and drew open a curtain at the corner of the room. She removed some items from behind it and, one by one, held them up in front of her. The clothes were skimpy to say the least – 'teddies, a negligeé and a see-through body stocking.

"My father buys me these," she said.

Thomas was shocked, embarrassed.

"Your father!" He wondered why he was supplying her with sexy underwear. Thomas needed an acceptable explanation for this strange relationship. He suddenly felt threatened by her father, and protective towards her but perhaps that was her intention. Perhaps she was lying, just being a bitch – she hadn't answered.

"And your mother – what does she say?" he asked, looking for a supportive point of view.

"My mother's dead," she replied, matter of factly, leaving him feeling even more awkward. Not replacing the lingerie, but leaving them hanging handily on a rail, she sat back on the floor. They both faced the television which was off.

"My father usually calls on a Sunday night."

Thomas immediately looked across at the door, but she reassured him.

"Don't worry," she said, "he's away this weekend."

He wanted to say something, anything, something comical to lighten the atmosphere but he was afraid he'd blow his chances by saying something wrong. Had the scar put her off? It was as if he was going down every snake in a game of snakes-and-ladders.

Thomas looked at her lips, full and just slightly parted – lips that suggested more than 'kiss me'. She was too close, there was no room to escape. He tried kissing her gently, open mouthed. To his surprise she moaned and softly bit his bottom lip. He released her teeth with his tongue and she returned his kiss, simultaneously pushing hard onto his hand which was already between her legs. Then, as soon as he had adjusted to her forcefulness, she pushed his hand away and pleaded, "Please, please don't tease me."

Confused, but with no such intention, he unzipped her jeans and, with her help, stripped her naked. He was so overwhelmed by her body that he forgot to take off any of his own clothes. She lay on her back across the bed, making no effort to cover herself and ordered him to undress. He undid the laces of his Dr Martens police boots, then he stood up straight, facing her, looking down at her as he undressed deliberately and unhurriedly, trying to concentrate, hanging on to what little control he had left.

"Are you just a PC? Why aren't you an Inspector, or on the CID, or something?" she taunted.

CID? What the hell did she know! He'd tried it for three months and hated it. No, all his friends and best times were in uniform and as for promotion – she wouldn't have approached him in a dance if he had been top brass. But had she said this to make him more aggressive? He didn't care. It suited him that way too and now, naked, he lay between her legs. But she stopped him again, pushing him away. This time she got off the bed and walked to her handbag, taking from it a bottle of baby oil which she handed to him. God, he thought! The boys will never believe this.

* * *

It was 1.30am as Thomas sat on the edge of the bed pulling his uniform trousers back on.

"Fine friend you turned out to be," he said, making a joke of her earlier statement. Again she failed to appreciate his sense of humour, saying, "I'm tired – make sure the downstairs door is properly closed when you leave."

He said, "Goodnight," leaving her uncovered on the bed and let himself out, making a note of her number as he passed the telephone on the kitchen wall. Thomas quietly walked onto the sleepy, silent street, the cold air catalizing her perfume which was in his pores. He noticed a plain-clothes policeman sitting in a car which he knew better than its present occupant. It was parked at the end of the road. Thomas had a futile hope that the detective hadn't seen him and as he walked passed he deliberately avoided looking at the car. But then he thought, 'I wonder if he's going to see her, if he's been waiting for me to leave so he could go up? Perhaps she's into policemen. Perhaps he's one of many.' His jealousy returned. Looking at his watch he thought to himself, 'God! is that the time?'

* * *

He was home by 2am and in bed, with his head swimming in the swirl of the evening's events. His wife stirred in bed next to him but didn't wake. His wife! Hell! What was she doing back? That was all he needed, a reconciliation.

Cathy had divorced to marry Thomas, but her ex-husband had won custody of their three-year-old son. She had coped for the first year, but slowly she became more and more distant from Thomas and told him it was because she was missing her baby. He had helped her to get access to the child, but that hadn't been enough. She would stay away for days on end, sometimes weeks, living with the boy and her ex-husband, and returning to Thomas in between. When he'd asked if she wanted a divorce she had only said no, and that he didn't understand her and to give her time. He loved her in his way and sympathised but just didn't know how to help her. Instead he had let her come and go as she pleased. Thomas missed her when she was away but – just as he got used to life without her, she'd turn up, usually at the most inappropriate time – like tonight. During one almighty row he'd threatened to put a big cat-flap in the door. But that had been unfair. She wasn't cheap, just torn by conflicting emotions. Now it seemed to be his turn again, but this time such ideas were definitely out. He sneaked downstairs to sleep, ready for a quick getaway in the morning.

CHAPTER TWO

At 9am Thomas was on duty at Gordonstow Police Station, brushing his uniform and checking the creases for sharpness. All policemen reserved a spare uniform for special occasions – Royal visits, court appearances, staff appraisals and bollockings – to be religiously stored away after each ritual like a lady's Sunday-best hat. This morning, dressed for a court appearance with their boots bulled and hair neatly combed, Thomas Cord and Richard Speak looked like boys many a mother would be proud to have as sons-in-law.

Richard was Thomas's partner and friend. That morning they were involved in the same case and, taking an opportunity to sneak off, they looked for a quiet room where they could hide undisturbed for half-an-hour and revise their pocket books. They tried the games-room on the top floor and found it suitably deserted. Empty plastic cups encircled the waste paper bin on the bare linoleum tiled floor where they had landed or rolled, after failing to reach their intended target. The ash trays, full of cigarette butts, had been left on the table-tennis table, two darts had been left in the dart board, one having fallen on the floor. The only thing which had been left reasonably tidy was the snooker table.

"We had better get out of here before the cleaners see the mess," said Richard. "They are going to play hell over this again."

The cleaners always complained to the senior officers about the untidiness of the boys on the beat and, to the disgust of the 'boys', the senior officers invariably upheld the cleaners' complaints, no matter how trivial, probably in fear of industrial action.

"It's not that bad," suggested Thomas, sitting on a cheap olive-green, PVC covered bench, which let out a hiss of air as it settled under him. Both he and Richard relaxed and read through their case.

After some quiet minutes it was Richard who broke the silence.

"How did you do with that piece you pulled the other night?"

"What piece is that, Speak?" Thomas replied.

"You know," he smiled.

"She's alright," Thomas conceded. "Why?"

"Oh, so you haven't met her lesbian friend yet?"

"No, has she got one then?"

"Yes, she's a doll, looks like her. You'd swear they were sisters."

Thomas thought about this. He wasn't a bit surprised to hear Pamela had a lesbian friend. Why not, she seemed to be into everything else. But he didn't feel jealous at another woman being a lover. Dismissing it, he looked at his watch and said, "It's ten, shall we go across to court?"

They got up and made a final check on their appearance before walking over to the magistrate's court. On the way out of the station, Thomas passed the same Detective Sergeant that had been parked watching the flat. Simultaneously they avoided each other's eyes. Thomas fleetingly thought of him in bed with Pamela and decided to go and see her at lunch-time.

Both PC's stepped out onto the street, squinting in the September morning sunshine, and were immediately joined by the duty Inspector from another uniformed squad, who was walking out to the car park. Thomas had worked with the Inspector on a number of occasions, and disliked his bombastic 'don't do as I do, do as I say' hypocritical manner.

"Good morning, gentlemen," he acknowledged.

"Good morning, sir," they replied in unison, not attempting anything as formal as a salute. "Lovely day."

"Yes, lovely day. What case have you two got on this morning?"

"Nothing much sir, just a breathalyser," Richard replied.

"Either of you got a match?" he asked, feeling his pockets.

"Don't smoke, sir," said Thomas. "Should have some in there though," indicating the paper shop across the road. All three crossed to the shop. Thomas opened the door and followed the Inspector inside.

"Get me a packet of chewing gum, Thomas," Richard said. "I'll pay you when I get change."

Thomas picked up two packets of chewing gum then noticed some contraceptives displayed on the counter. He took a packet out of the display and slipped it onto the box of matches the Inspector had left on the counter as he browsed through the headlines, waiting to pay. Thomas didn't wait. He gave the correct money for the chewing gums to the woman assistant, who had just finished tidying some magazines, and went out. As he joined Richard outside, he turned to see the Inspector, red-faced as the assistant tried to charge him for the condoms.

Thomas told Richard what he'd done as they hurried across to the court and they were still laughing as they reached the bottom of the steps. It was then Thomas realised that he had forgotten his dummy – he had left it in his other tunic. Regularly the squads would try to raise money for charity amongst themselves – usually a local cause. The most popular way they found to do this was by playing a type of forfeit game. The rules were simple. For a period every officer, while on duty, would have to do a certain pre-agreed thing when challenged by a colleague. If he failed to do it, then he would have to forfeit one pound to the charity. If he did do it then the challenger would have to forfeit the pound. The last challenge, 'Bobble Cap!' had required a woollen bobble cap to be donned, irrespective of how unlikely the circumstances might been at the time. Thomas had been challenged whilst on point duty directing traffic and had lifted his helmet to reveal the bobble cap underneath. This week, if one of the boys shouted, 'Dummy', the challenged squad member would have to put a dummy in his mouth!

Just like one of those bastards to shout it out when I'm in the witness box, Thomas thought, and refrained from mentioning it to Richard in case it gave him ideas. If the chance came about, he'd do it to Richard though! By 1pm the opportunity hadn't arisen but the case was over and Thomas was in a hurry to go off duty early in order to see Pamela. He left Richard to go on ahead and followed a gaggle of traffic wardens entering the station for their lunch, grabbed his civilian jacket, changed, and by five past one was walking up the steps to the hair salon, the smell of the perm solution and the noise of the driers making him aware that it was a busy day. He felt apprehensive but went in. Three customers, isolated by their driers, heads perfectly still, followed him with their eyes, speculating at this male intrusion, but the staff smiled knowingly at him and one, a good-looking blonde of about forty-five, called over to Pamela who was just taking payment from a Princess Di look-a-like. Pamela came over and, from the girlish atmosphere in the salon, he was sure that there had been a briefing on the previous night's performance. One or two of the young ones actually looked him up and down, eyes lingering on his flies. He discretely positioned himself so that he could look across into a mirror to check his zip wasn't undone. Even when not in full uniform there was nothing worse than a policeman walking about with his flies open!

Pamela came across, looking attractive but tired.

"I'm going for a coffee," she said, "Do you want to come? Only, I can't stay long. I've got to nip into town."

"That's alright," Thomas said, as he opened the door of the salon for her. "I have to go to town as well. I need to buy some clay and Plaster of Paris."

"What on earth for – casting a burglar's footprint?" she asked.

"No," he replied, "I sculpt."

"Oh, yeh. What particularly?" asked Pamela, somewhat intrigued.

"Well, horses mainly, but I do occasionally sculpt women, you know – figures."

"Are you any good at doing horses?" she asked, still not sure whether to believe him or not.

"Well, not really. I can't get my leg over," he said, smiling.

"You know what I mean," she replied, impatient with what she considered to be childish humour.

"Well, I've had six commissions of race horses which I've done in bronze and they've all been recommendations. Here, I've got some photographs you can see," he said, taking them from his jacket pocket.

"Hey! These are marvellous," she said, enthusiastically studying them closely and now stopping in the street.

"How do you get the different highlights and colours in the bronze?"

"That's all done with chemicals. I'll show you one day if you like."

"How much would one of these cost?" she asked.

"About £1,000, depending on how much travelling I have to do. It's the casting though that's the biggest expense, being just a one-off."

"Yes, I realize that," she said, still admiring the photographs.

"Can you do one for me?"

"What, at £1,000?"

"Of course," she answered. "I'm not poor you know. That's my hairdressing salon. I own it."

"OK I'm sorry, keep your hair on." Thomas was relieved that she hadn't expected him to do it for nothing. "Yes, I'll do one for you – whose horse?"

"It's my father's horse, actually. I want it for a surprise on his birthday at the end of October. Will you be able to do it by then. I'll pay you in advance?"

He thought a moment.

"I'm in the middle of a sculpture of a head at the moment, but there's no rush on that – I can put it aside. That gives me over a month and if I'm lucky enough to get him right first time then yes, I might be able to manage it. You still haven't told me who the horse is?"

"It's Eyecatcher."

"What! *The* Eyecatcher?" he said, with surprise.

"Yes."

"Of course! Thatchit Corran owns that. Did he name it after your behind?" asked Thomas, stepping back to have an appreciative look at her rear.

"Get lost," she snapped.

"Hey, come on," he said, trying to change her mood.

"You're quite immature really, I'm already getting bored with you."

He wasn't sure how to take this. Did she mean it or was it another of her wind-ups, leading to a good, hard repeat session? The fact that it was lunchtime wouldn't have mattered to her, but she solved the problem for him.

"I've got one of my periods coming and I'm not in the mood for your humour. Let's get a coffee and I'll write you a cheque."

"You don't have to pay me yet," Thomas said.

"I want to," she replied. "I'll know then that it will be done."

"Fair enough," Thomas accepted, "is there any particular way you'd like him?"

"Come," she said, "let's go into Gershwin's and discuss it."

They found a table by the window and Thomas ordered two coffees with cream.

"I'd like to do him with that aloof look he's got," he suggested.

"Yes," she said, thoughtfully, "if you could capture that, then one couldn't deny the sculpture was of him. Good idea."

He was pleased she agreed. He loved working on horses and judged his success on capturing their form and idiosyncracies.

Pamela wrote out the cheque and drank her coffee.

"I must go," she said, getting up. She handed him the cheque. He remained seated, not wanting the meeting to break up so soon.

"Will I see you tonight?" he asked.

"I don't know," she said, trying to put him off.

"I'll ring you," he suggested.

"No, ring me the day after tomorrow. I'm sleeping at my friend's tonight."

With this she walked away, leaving Thomas to pay the bill.

Thomas looked at the cheque before folding it into his pocket. The seventh commission, he thought. Mum will be nagging me again to follow her example and turn professional. Everything he knew of sculpting he'd learnt from her; even as a small child he would prefer to play with a lump of clay than a paint brush, standing by her as she worked, watching every creative move. Even at four it was far easier for him to attempt to model a horse than try drawing a matchstick man or house; he smiled at the thought of his mother still treasuring his first effort, a five legged animal, the fifth being the tail, with a head stuck on the body without a neck and the back legs bending forward at the knees like a human.

He'd come a long way since then. Having a successful equine sculptress for a mother had made it a lot easier; they both loved working on horses but, for him, it was racehorses. It was the unique combination of power and grace he found irresistible, but no, he couldn't be a professional. He was afraid his love for the work would wane if forced by commitment. He began to plan ahead in his mind. He'd need photographs and he'd need to spend time with the horse. That was no problem – he knew the stable girl. She was his best pal, lover, mother, sister, all rolled into one. No woman had ever got closer to him. Summer Wells was now twenty-nine and looked a lot younger. She had given birth at fifteen and was an unmarried mother, deserted by the father of Adam, her boy, before he'd been born. Demanding nothing of each other, she got on well with Thomas and found him amusing company and dirty in bed. Summer had the figure of a ballet dancer; firm and well balanced with big doe eyes and hair so long that she could sit on it. Often she had stroked it along his entire naked body, a privileged, sexual sensation. Everything was right between them and they were always comfortable in each other's company. As their relationship developed they often found that they picked up each other's thoughts. She had uncannily guessed that Thomas's scar had been the result of a school accident and was amused by his nickname but never used it, finding 'Doorstop' too much of a mouthful. Thomas wouldn't have minded; he especially liked her humour. Summer was broad-minded, multi-talented, well-read and intelligent, adventurous in bed and could use make-up like a photographer's model. In spite of being a musician and a photographer herself she settled for working with horses. The hours were convenient for her and, with the help of her parents, she was able to meet the needs of her son and earn a little more than she'd get on the dole, the only alternative if she was going to live at home. Summer looked after three horses, one of which was Eyecatcher.

Thomas telephoned her, not sure if she'd be home at Lambourn, but she answered.

"This is an obscene telephone call," he breathed.

"Thomas!" she exclaimed, laughing.

"Balls," he said, thinking he had disguised his voice well enough. "Can I come up and see you tonight?"

"Of course you can, about eight o'clock and bring your camera."

"Which one?" he asked.

"The Polaroid," Summer answered, "I'm in the mood!"

* * *

Approaching home, he remembered Cath, his wife. With each reunion being cooler than the last, he dreaded the thought of having to face her yet again but, as he entered, a tidied home and a note told him not to expect to see her for another week.

At 6pm he tried Pamela's number. He wouldn't have known what to say if she answered, but he just wanted to see if she had been telling him the truth about not being in that night. There was no reply. He tried again at 7 and then at 7.30 – still no reply. He let it ring while he set the video timer for a programme he was sure to miss if he was going to take his Polaroid to Summer's. Satisfied that Pamela was out he put down the receiver, got into his car and set off. Twenty minutes later Buster the Alsatian announced Thomas's arrival at Summer's before he reached the front door. Summer opened it for him after a quick glance through the curtains to check who was there.

"Hi," she greeted, pleased to see him, "I've only just got in before you. Adam's at a schoolfriend's house for the night – they've just left."

As Thomas walked in he asked, "Have you eaten?"

"No."

"I've brought some chilli con carne I made, from the freezer," he said, holding up a plastic carrier bag. "If you don't fancy it tonight it'll keep for a day or two."

"Mmm . . . that's fine, only what about the garlic?"

"If we both eat it we won't smell it, will we?" he said, nose right up to hers.

She kissed him fully on the mouth, not letting him say any more. She wanted him tonight. Thomas went into the kitchen to prepare the food, putting the chilli in the microwave to defrost, while Summer went upstairs for a bath. She had already showered at the stables before coming home but still felt the need to bathe herself and make up for the night ahead.

There wasn't much for Thomas to do. He wasn't going to start the spaghetti until he heard the bath plug pulled. He put on a record of Sixties Soul music and, singing along with Smokey Robinson, loosened his collar button, kicked off his shoes and slumped on the settee. He felt so at home here. The photographs on the wall led his eyes around the room. They were mostly of Summer's friends and couldn't be described as snaps for they captured the mood and originality one learnt to expect from Summer's camera. She was forever rearranging, replacing these photos with new ones. There was one of him sculpting and another of him in uniform giving a wink.

All the photographs were in black and white, matching the decor and furnishings. She had used very little colour in this room. But the plain pastels of the photo frames picked out the colour in the vase of flowers on the black piano to very good effect. It was chic and made the room look quite large for a small house.

His eyes settled on a photograph album on the coffee table. He picked it up and browsed through. In contrast it contained coloured photographs of Eyecatcher and showed his every quirk, from his aloof expression to his long sweeping canter. Through all his paces, this horse had stage presence, poise and grace and his walk was that of a toe-pointing prima ballerina. You couldn't teach Eyecatcher anything that could improve him. He was the complete horse, the ultimate. His many predecessors had been described at best as well-oiled machines, but nobody called Eyecatcher a machine – he had brains. He had won all his ten races; four as a two-year-old followed by the 2000 Guineas, the Derby, King George and Queen Elizabeth Stakes, the St

Ledger and The Prix de l'Arc de Triomphe, and now as a four-year-old he had gained a repeat win in this year's King George and Queen Elizabeth Stakes, in record time and from this year's record breaking Derby winner. No horse had ever been rated higher in Timeform, yet in all his races he had not won by more than a head.

Eyecatcher knew exactly who he was and what he was at the races for. On training gallops he would push himself to the utmost, causing his trainer to criticize the works rider on more than one occasion for not riding to instructions, but Eyecatcher wasn't being ridden – he was training himself. On the big day, the race itself, he'd run again as he wanted, his jockey being just a privileged passenger, a witness to tell the stories and hand down the legend. Eyecatcher would run alongside whichever horse was in front. If another horse came alongside with a challenge then he'd run alongside that one, just keeping pace, actually looking at him. As soon as the winning post was twenty yards away he'd change his pace and quicken up so effortlessly that he'd pass the post with just enough to spare and then look back at the second as a confident jockey would as he drew away. This was not a machine but a living legend. Thomas had thought of sculpting the horse running and looking back but it was so unnatural that he thought it would look too far-fetched. After all, a horse had a very wide field of vision, why should he need to turn his head. Now Thomas had seen the sculpture he wanted to do and Summer had captured it for him – the paddock walk. As he studied the photograph in more detail Summer came downstairs into the room. Thomas suddenly remembered the food. As he stood up to go to the kitchen she gently pushed him back into the chair, her bath robe opening, revealing stockings, suspenders and the secret of the evening she had planned.

"We'll eat later," she whispered, his reply suffocated in her enveloping mouth as the Eyecatcher album slid to the floor.

Exactly twenty minutes later Summer quickly kissed Thomas on the tip of his nose and said, "Right. I'm starving. Let's have food."

He eased himself up from the floor and watched as she picked up his clothes, passing them to him. He noticed the bite mark on her back which he had seen earlier, during their lovemaking. He hadn't referred to it then. It had flashed past in his mind as she had brought him orally to a climax.

"How did you get that bite on your back? You want to choose your boyfriends more carefully," not wanting to sound jealous but commenting out of genuine concern.

"Oh, that! The new horse I've been given to look after gave it to me a couple of days ago."

"A gypsy once told me that if a horse bites you, you should bite his tongue and he won't do it again," Thomas said.

"Who was that? A gypsy without a nose?" she asked mockingly.

"Well, that's what he said."

"OK, if it does it again, I'll give you a shout and you can bite its tongue for me," she said, biting his tongue.

"Come on – get your clothes on. I'm starving."

Thomas wasn't long serving the food and they sat at a table which Summer had romantically prepared with flowers and candles. Now in a simple black mini-dress, she poured the wine.

"How long have you had another horse to look after?" Thomas asked her.

"Oh! of course, I haven't told you have I?" she said, remembering. "There's been a shift-about with Eyecatcher. He's been moved to another box, separate to the main block, one with security cameras, sound sensors, the lot, and I've been given this rogue Pillow Talk to look after instead. I suppose he's just a big baby really, but he'll come all right."

Summer didn't seem that disappointed so Thomas pressed her.

"Who is Eyecatcher's lad now then?"

"Serge Ravir," she replied.

"Sounds French," he said.

"Telling me!" said Summer. "Doesn't speak a word of English – nice bum though."

"You mean he *is* French?" Thomas said, emphasizing the *is*.

"Yeah, it's only Mr Best who speaks to him," she clarified.

"But I thought Eric Best promised you that as long as he trained Eyecatcher then you would be his lad."

"He did," Summer answered, "but it's out of his hands. Mr Corran is supposed to have brought Ravir over. Talk is he's been borrowed from stables not far from Laon because of his familiarity with the French racing scene. None of us are really comfortable when we're abroad."

"But why all the sudden fuss with security and all. I know he's odds-on already for the Arc, but he was last year as well and there wasn't all this fuss," Thomas argued.

"Well, rumour is that there've been death threats made against 'Catch' ," she said.

"How certain are you?" asked Thomas.

"I don't know. It could be one of Corran's ideas to get more publicity – that man basks in publicity. God, he's so false. I suppose he'll manipulate a big build-up story right up until the Arc."

Thomas still wasn't satisfied.

"What I can't understand is why Corran wants to run Eyecatcher again in the Arc anyway. He won it last year beating the best of all ages after being unbeaten all season and then, having his first run as a four-year-old, beat the best of this and last season's cream by winning the King George and Queen Elizabeth stakes for the second year running. I mean, he's got nothing to prove by winning the Arc again. Surely, Corran would be wiser retiring him now while he's still unbeaten."

"But he's not owned by Thatchit Corran. He's only leased by him and it's only a three season contract," Summer explained.

"I didn't know that," Thomas said incredulously. "I always thought the horse was his."

"So do most people," said Summer, "and that's because he named the horse in conjunction with his cosmetic company. It will be amusing to learn what he'll be naming his next horse. He's manufacturing cosmetics for men now – or rather cosmetics for gay men."

"I see," said Thomas, "so in fact what he's after from another Arc win is extra advertising and a few thousand pounds in prize money."

"Four-hundred-and-twenty-three thousand to be exact," Summer pointed out, "and from what I hear he desperately needs it."

"You're kidding! He's worth millions."

"I don't know so much. You'd know more about that than me, only – I know – you're not supposed to say because you're a policeman," she said mockingly.

"Honestly," he said, with all sincerity, "I didn't know any of this. What you've told me is all news to me."

He was telling the truth but the look on his face didn't fully convince her. It was often the case in his job that members of the public knew more about certain matters than some of the police themselves, news having more freedom to get around the street than it would by the internal force grapevine. This was also true if someone was being secretly investigated, but what he found most embarrassing was when he'd been off for the weekend and something would appear in the paper or on the news which he knew absolutely nothing about and he'd be quizzed on it in his local pub. They always thought he was holding back.

"Who really does own Eyecatcher then, Summer?"

"I don't know any names," she said, "only it's the stud farm that bred him. Why do you want to know?"

"Well, I've been commissioned to do a sculpture of him and I don't know if I'll be allowed to now."

"Of course you will. After all nothing's changed, only your knowledge about it that's all."

"I suppose you're right," he said, comforted.

"Anyway, what's this about a commission?" she asked excitedly.

"Pamela Corran asked me to . . ." Before he could finish, Summer spluttered and began to cough.

"Ooh, this chilli's hot." She reached for the wine and as she drank deeply her throat got hotter. He started to laugh, realizing her mistake in drinking to try and cool her mouth.

"My lips are numb. God, you don't half make it hot."

He knew the mention of Pamela had triggered the cough but played along.

"It's nice though," she managed to say when she got her feeling back. "Mmm . . . but Christ, it's hot."

"Who, Pamela?" he joked.

"No, the chilli, you twit. Oh, no! You haven't bonked her have you?" Summer was now back on course.

"More like she bonked me."

"I believe that," Summer replied, wiping her nose with a tissue. "She used to be in school with me until she got herself expelled and a teacher sacked. Well, well, well - you and Pamela Corran."

"It's nothing serious," Thomas said, now feeling a bit exposed. Summer was enjoying this and continued, "What was it this time, her bum?"

"How did you know?"

"I know you better than you know yourself. Suzanne Danielle's legs, Annie Lennox's smile and now Pamela Corran's bum."

"There's no harm in dreaming," he said defensively.

"You just said she bonked you," Summer reiterated,

"Oh, she did. It's just that I see beauty in everyone," he protested.

"All you see is a good bonk, more like," she smiled, now looking with a knowing amusement into his eyes.

"Has anyone ever told you that you've got Atlantic eyes?"

"What?" he said, half tilting his head in case he'd misheard. "Atlantic eyes! What the hell are Atlantic eyes?"

"Oh, nothing," she said, still amused. "The less you know about them the better." She stood up to do the dishes. Thomas followed her to help, looking at his eyes as he passed the mirror but he couldn't see what she meant.

Having cleared up, Thomas sat on the settee with Summer curled up by his knees on the floor. She lay the album in front of her and slowly turned over her photographs of Eyecatcher.

"You can borrow these if they are any good to you."

Again, he thought, she had anticipated. So easy to get on with.

"Please," he said enthusiastically, "they'd save me no end of time. Will you mention it to Eric for me so that I can arrange with him to come up and see the horse. I need that to get the depth and subtleness that's missed in two dimensions."

"OK, I'll tell him. Anyway you know that Eric will do all he can for you. He likes you and your work – sculptures, that is. Right, now it's your turn."

She got up, handed him his Polaroid and dropped her dress.

"How do you want me?"

CHAPTER THREE

The following day's tour of duty started at 2pm. Thomas and Richard were together, driving around the town.

"What have you got on this afternoon, Rich?" Thomas asked.

"Nothing much. I'm trying to wind down. I don't want to get involved in anything. I'll be starting my holidays tomorrow. Will you keep an eye on the flat while I'm away? The spare key's in my locker."

"Yeh, OK. Decided where you're going yet?"

"Usual piss-up in Marbella."

"Lucky sod," Thomas said, looking a bit sick.

"Where are you going?" Richard asked.

"I don't know yet."

Thomas hadn't thought of going away. "I've got do a sculpture. Probably nowhere. That reminds me," he said with renewed interest. "Have you heard anything about Thatchit Corran?"

"Your future father-in-law?" Richard smirked.

"Piss off," Thomas said, pulling up at the red lights.

"Sorry, I couldn't resist that," said Richard. "As it happens, I was snooping around in the fraud squad office one night shift and I saw a report answering a request from Interpol to look into his business interests, although I don't think it helped them much."

"What did it say?" Thomas asked impatiently.

He looked in his mirror and moved off as the lights turned to green, trying to listen above the background conversations on the police radio.

"From what I can remember," Richard began, "it was something to do with one of his make-up lines. He's apparently been launching a new designer eye make-up which is supposed to be natural, you know, organic and all that, non-allergic I suppose. Anyway, I think it's called 'Smudge'. What's happened is that loads of people have invested in little cottage industries making this stuff in Northern France. They've been producing the base ingredient for months and tons have been made."

"So what's wrong in that?" Thomas quizzed.

"Nothing on the face of it – excuse the pun," Richard continued, "it's just that the way the whole thing's been set up makes it look like a big scale con-trick. Very clever but legal."

Thomas stopped the car so that he could concentrate.

"It's over a month now since I saw the report," Richard continued, "but from what I can remember it's this; Corran employs French salesmen or reps to visit farms and cottages in Northern France, asking if they would be interested in producing a simple product for which they'd be handsomely paid. If they're interested, and let's face it who wouldn't be, they're told that for an investment of five hundred pounds or the equivalent in francs they would receive one hundred live cultures, a necessary ingredient to commence production. Each culture, which is supposed to look like a cardboard scab when grown, is broken in two halves and each half is put to float on a glass of milk for four weeks, where it grows to cover the surface, thickening to its original size."

"What is it made of?" Thomas interrupted.

"I don't know," Richard answered, "but I should imagine it's just like yoghurt or curd from milk separation because it's then taken off the top of the milk – which must be honking by now – and dried. The one culture is then sold back to Corran who promises by way of contract to buy it back at two pounds fifty while the other is retained and split to repeat the process. So after eight weeks the producer has recovered his investment of five hundred pounds and after that he is making two hundred and fifty pounds per month for every hundred cultures he's bought. The only ongoing expense he's got is for the milk and the glasses, but as most of them are farmers anyway the milk is no problem."

"What's to stop a producer from breaking them into four and making more cultures?" Thomas asked.

"The contract," Richard said. "Corran will only take the same number as those initially purchased. He keeps a record of what he should expect from the producer and won't accept any more. He says this ensures the consistency of the product."

"It sounds as easy as printing money to me," Thomas said. "Is five hundred pounds the most one can invest?"

"It was at first," Richard said, "but as more and more producers were taken on then many expanded, reinvesting their profits."

"What does Corran do with all this stuff?"

"Well, he's told the producers that the cakes are crushed into a powder which is made into a base paste for the make-up, ready for shipping to Britain and the States."

"Do you realize how much money Corran is making out of this?" said Thomas. "If he can keep finding new producers all he needs to do is supply them with the cultures produced for him by the others at double the price. It would work like a chain letter. You're talking about literally millions of pounds in a very short time."

"I know," replied Richard.

"But," said Thomas, "there's going to be a time when he's going to saturate the market and that's going to cause problems."

"That time's arrived already," said Richard. "At first, every one was raking it in, counting the days when their mortgages would be paid off. However, after the early months, Corran wasn't collecting and the later producers who'd climbed on the band-waggon have been left high and dry with no return whatsoever on whopping investments."

"So that's why the big Interpol investigation?" suggested Thomas.

"You've got it in one," replied Richard, "but Corran's been clever. He's retained a warehouse full of this paste in Southampton and told the fraud squad that he's experiencing a problem getting the make-up marketed. So he's sitting pretty, not having sold one iota of the stuff for make-up but he's already sold the producers the privilege of making it at astronomic profits for himself."

"Incredible!" Thomas was impressed. "The man's a bloody genius," he said.

"No, a millionaire," said Richard, "but boy, he must have a million enemies to go with it. You see, there's another twist to this. Every one is hoping that they'll get their money back. Some are still hoping to make fortunes and they are living in hope that this is only a temporary hiccup. Even those who smell a rat are not making a complaint because they know that if the company folds they can say goodbye to their cash for good. They are up to their necks in debt and cultures."

"Would this stuff be any good as a make-up then?" Thomas asked as an afterthought.

"Don't bloody ask me. Never use the stuff," Richard said.

"That reminds me. Do you remember the time we raided that gay club when the Sergeant insisted on going first and they thought he was the kissogram?"

"I'll never forget his face."

Reminding themselves of that always reduced them to laughter.

"Going back to Pamela," said Thomas, changing the subject. "Did you know her old man buys her lingerie?" This fact was still bothering him.

"Well, I suppose he does – indirectly," said Richard. "Daddy pays for everything – he dotes on her. If she wants lingerie she probably phones him and he tells her to help herself. Why? Oh, you thought there's something going on between them, didn't you?"

"Well, it had crossed my mind," confessed Thomas.

"She's just having you on – stoking you up, mate.

Don't listen to her. She's got too many boyfriends for that nonsense."

"Fancy a cup of tea?" said Thomas, a little happier now.

"OK, where?" agreed Richard, thinking it was a good idea.

"I've got to go to Full Road to return some property to this old dear. We'll have one there."

Full Road was only two streets away. He started the car and they were there in minutes. As they arrived Richard said, "Don't forget to lock the car. You don't want the same thing to happen to us as the CID."

"What was that?" said Thomas.

"They were taking some stolen property back to Ali's garage in Church Street. He was so grateful he insisted on giving them a drink each. Well, he kept them for more than an hour, not that they minded, with all the booze and a home-made curry. They drove back to the station half-cut and then the Inspector drew their attention to a sunroof that had been fitted in the CID car! Old Ali had done it to show his gratitude."

"Oh no," said Thomas, laughing. "Are they on a charge?"

"You bet," said Richard.

Picturing the situation, they were still laughing as they reached Mrs Evans's door. It was – as Thomas usually found it – wide open.

"Come in lovely boys," she welcomed, as they put their heads around the doorway. "Do you want a drink?"

Mrs Evans was a stout, shiny-faced woman of about seventy, wearing a fresh floral pinafore to cover her plain brown woollen clothes. She showed them both into a small room where every conceivable place to sit was occupied by a cat. The TV was blaring.

"Well, it's nice to see you. Sit down," she said. "I don't think I've met you before," she looked at Richard, offering her hand.

"I beg your pardon, Mrs Evans. This is my colleague, PC Speak."

"Pleased to meet you," Richard said, raising his voice and, with politeness, gently shaking the proffered hand. She smiled.

"You'll have to speak up dear, a bit deaf I am."

Richard had thought as much.

"Hold on," she said, "I'll turn this up." She fiddled with her deaf aid, leaving the television as it was. "Now that's better," she said relaxing. "What did you say you wanted to drink?"

Richard shouted over the unrelenting television newscaster, "Thanks, I'll have a coffee, milk no sugar."

"And you dear?" Mrs Evans turned to Thomas. "You can help yourself, you know where it is. Take two." Happy to have guests, she disappeared towards the kitchen.

Thomas walked across the bare hall into a sparsely furnished room. The floor was untidily piled with boxes of account books, worming powder, old vet's posters, horse remedies, forms, horse bandages, the lot; papers were scattered everywhere but neatly stacked in a corner were four polythene-covered, twenty-four can packs of lager, the top one already opened. He only took one – he was driving. Returning to join Richard, he rearranged a cat, made room and sat down.

"You made a mistake there, Rich," he said.

"What?" Richard shouted. "Jesus, I'm going bloody deaf myself with this TV on." He reached over and turned it down.

"You made a mistake," Thomas shouted.

"How do you mean?" said Richard, looking a little worried.

"She dunks her biscuits in her coffee and doesn't wash the cups properly. You'll probably find lumps at the bottom."

Richard thought Thomas was kidding but wasn't sure. He swallowed and thought of changing his order but it was too late. Carefully carrying a cup, Mrs Evans returned.

"There you are, lovely, hope it is alright, try it." She handed him the cup and waited until he took a sip.

"Cheers," Thomas chuckled, raising his can to his mouth. A silent Richard looked across at him and sneered.

"That's lovely. Thanks, Mrs Evans," he said, after a forced swallow.

"You'll have to speak up," she said, turning to Thomas. "Isn't he shy? Well, it's nice to see you. You haven't been here for over a week."

Thomas glanced at Richard, who was looking none too healthy, his eyes searching for somewhere to pour away the coffee. Thomas knew the cups were perfectly clean. Mrs Evans didn't dunk her biscuits but she did use powdered milk and never stirred it in properly, leaving lumps at the bottom. He chuckled to himself but covered it as he replied to Mrs Evans.

"I've got a surprise for you."

"What is it?" she said, half expecting a joke – he often teased her.

"Well, have you lost anything?"

She patted around herself, checking for her spectacles which she found hanging on a chain around her neck. "No, I don't think so, why?"

Thomas handed her a purse.

"Good gosh, where did you find that?" she exclaimed, putting her hands up to her face.

"You left it in the Post Office this morning. They tried to telephone you but couldn't get an answer."

"That's funny," she said, "I didn't hear it ring."

Thomas made her check the contents and sign his property receipt book.

"Do you want more coffee?" she said to Richard, who was still struggling over a brew that was becoming cold as well as lumpy. He looked into the cup and saw it was not all liquid. Unable to swallow what was in his mouth he tried to shake his head but choked and began to cough. She misheard what she thought to be a yes and took his cup from him, in order to fill it up.

"Oh, you've still got some left."

"Oscar Three One. Control to Oscar Three One." At that point a saving voice on the pocket radio diverted their attention.

"Go ahead to Oscar Three One," Thomas replied.

The voice returned. "Will you attend to a damage-only accident in Blue Stone Road. The road is blocked. I'll send another car to assist you."

Richard blew out a sigh of relief. Thomas swallowed the last of his lager and stood up. "I'm sorry, Mrs Evans love, but we've got to go – an accident."

"I hope nobody's hurt," she said, seeing them to the door, "and thank you for bringing my purse."

Outside, Thomas walked on ahead of Richard, unlocked the car, got in and started the engine as Richard joined him.

"You bastard," Richard said as Thomas, the tears streaming down his cheeks, tried to say that it was only powdered milk but the words kept getting lost in his laughter. They drove on and it was Richard, with a small grin of forgiveness, who first changed the subject.

"I thought that was a vet's surgery?"

"It was," Thomas replied, "Jed Evans's – that was his mother. He concentrates on horses these days though and, although eccentric, he's gained great respect in the racing fraternity."

"Racing's not my cup of tea," Richard said, disinterestedly.

"Or coffee," Thomas said, laughing again.

"But why is the place in such a mess?" Richard asked.

"It's always been the same. That's how they are. He bought a plot to build on about five years ago but it's got no further. I mean, he's not short of money obviously and there's just the two of them. Perhaps that's it, or maybe his mother doesn't want to move, but if they had a new place it would be in the same state pretty soon. Beats me how he can find anything, but she's a great old soul."

The accident, when they reached it, was routine and they made sure to leave the scene in time for their break.

* * *

The second-half of the shift left Thomas in the station with the daunting task of catching up on his paperwork. No-one liked paperwork – it was the worst part of the job. Statements weren't so bad, but there was a form or a card or booklet specifically designed for nearly every conceivable occurrence. There were no less than forty-two separate forms dealing with the new tape-recorded interview procedures alone. This stationery paraphernalia, after being requisitioned from the station administration department, was kept in large filing cabinets, accessible to all in what was commonly known as the parade room, so called because, at the start of each shift, it was the place where the squad would congregate to be addressed by their duty sergeant or inspector or anyone else such as the CID who had anything to tell them.

The parades didn't have to be held in this room but, with the ever-changing internal policies of the police force, a room never retained the purpose for which it was designed for long. Even the canteen had been moved twice since Thomas had been stationed there and the only places, as far as he could remember, which had enjoyed a permanent location, were the toilets and telephone switchboard room.

The cells, although permanent fixtures, were sometimes individually used for the secure storage of stolen property and, on one memorable occasion, one was occupied by three hundred confiscated cannabis plants. Six feet tall, uprooted and drying in the central heating, they released their heady musky aroma into the air and, by the end of two weeks, there wasn't a police officer in the station who wasn't an expert at identifying the smell of the drug.

The parade room was off a draughty corridor downwind from the cells and, in the early hours of the morning, with the central heating full on, would invariably harbour the stench of feet, urine and nervous sweat from the overnight prisoners. This evening, in spite of the one drunk in custody, the windows were open and the air was a little fresher.

Thomas shut the door in an effort to keep out the noise of the drunk who was repeatedly banging his cell door. The room boasted only the bare essentials, a bare wooden block floor, secondary double glazing and hospital gloss-painted walls, their clinical boredom broken only by duty rosters and court lists. These were taped weekly to the wall next to the only permanent fixture – a notice board. The reason why the rosters and court lists were taped to the wall was obvious – the notice board was full, full of small ads for anything from a Mini car to a space invader game.

Thomas had a quick look to see if any new cartoons had been pinned up and smiled to himself as he remembered what Richard had said about the CID car with the sunshine roof, but he was disappointed. There were none. The drawings, excellent in capturing character, were never signed. They were always about internal matters, very personal and down to earth. The humour often took advantage of some poor sod's demeanour, especially if they had made a cock-up, and no-one, irrespective of gender or rank, was spared. Thomas luckily hadn't been up there for two years but remembered the last time.

He'd been detailed to ride the first police pushbike the station had got as part of the new 'more policemen on the beat' policy. To save his embarrassment, he had left it parked in the town and walked the beat instead, but when he returned to it about an hour later, he had found it a total wreck. A lorry had reversed over it and driven off, unaware of the accident, leaving Thomas the uncomfortable task of having to explain why the Chief was now without his pride and joy.

As well as the steel stationery cabinets, a large table, covered in pen-knifed initials, and three rickety, hard, wooden chairs completed the furnishings. He picked the safest of them and settled down to do his reports. After a couple of hours he was interrupted by Pat Kleen, a policewoman who was in the traffic department and, including the men, was the best driver in the station. She and Thomas had worked together before she'd gone on to traffic and they'd got on well. He had found her pretty, black-eyed looks more a help than a hindrance and had often put his trust in her femininity rather than his physical power when trying to break up a fight.

"Hi, Doorstop," she said as she looked through the filing cabinet for an accident booklet. "Skiving again?" She was kidding. They had always privately slagged each other. That's how they got on without any bad feeling festering between them.

"Skiving!" he answered, "I've got a shed full of paperwork here. If I don't get it done now before my rest-day I won't know where I am."

"I'll leave you in peace then," she said. "You don't happen to have an accident booklet on you do you? There's none in the drawer."

He found one in his pocket and gave it to her. "Yeah, here." She took it.

"Bit bent, but it'll do, thanks. We're all going for a

drink tonight down the Ram, are you coming?"

Thomas let out a sigh, "No, Pat, I'm shattered. Thanks all the same."

"Well, if you change your mind, you'll know where we'll be." She turned and went out, giving him a little finger-wave.

At 9.30 Thomas cleared away his papers and reports before the cavalry charge of the shift change-over, and at 10 both he and Richard were off duty.

"Fancy a pint?" Richard asked.

"No, not for me mate. Pat asked me earlier. I'm shattered.'

"Too much bed and not enough sleep, that's your trouble," Richard joked.

"I'll see you after your holidays. Have a good time," Thomas said, walking away. It was no joke – he had to have an early night.

CHAPTER FOUR

The rest of the week was busy. On one shift alone Thomas had three arrests for criminal damage and one for a take and drive away. Three criminal damages in one night was not that unusual, but there were some really bizarre times; once he had had to deal with the only four pedestrian crossing accidents of the year, all in the same week and all on different crossings. Two had resulted in deaths. There seemed to be patches like this in every policeman's year where particular types of incidents appeared to be concentrated and it almost had him believing in the stars.

A week of solid crime had drained Thomas, and, by Thursday he was ready for two days off. As an excuse, he telephoned Pamela to ask if she wanted to come down to the stables with him to see Eyecatcher.

"Not likely," she said, "horses give me hay fever. Anyway, I've got to open – Friday's a busy day."

"Fancy lunch then?" he suggested.

"No thanks, I'm on a diet," was the curt reply.

"Will I see you again?" he asked.

"I don't think so. You're married. Just do me the sculpture." She put the phone down.

"Married," he thought. "Some marriage!"

He dialled Pamela's number again.

"Sorry," he said, "I got cut off."

"Look, there's no point in this," she answered. "I made a mistake, OK?"

"OK," he finally said, "I'll be in touch about the bronze."

"Right, bye bye," she replied, a little softer, and put down the receiver.

He was sorry, sorry he'd phoned her again. She sounded angry and bored. There was only one way to get seduced by her again and that was by doing the best sculpture he had ever done.

He immediately telephoned Eagle Lodge and spoke to Eric Best.

"Eric, it's Thomas."

"Hello Thomas, you've caught me at a busy time. How are you?"

Thomas was used to this from trainers.

"I've been right around the clock trying to phone you when you're not busy, and the only times you aren't must be the ones when you don't answer."

"What?" Eric said, bewildered.

"Oh, never mind," said Thomas. "Can I come down this morning? I want to see Eyecatcher. Pamela Corran has asked me to do a sculpture of him but don't tell her father – it's for his birthday."

"Sure, come down. See you in, what – half an hour?"

"About that, OK. Thanks. See you."

Thomas began to gather the materials he'd need to start the sculpture; pipe-cleaner, thin steel rods, pliers, a small hack-saw, tape, narrow bandages, a sketch pad and pencil just in case he'd have to make notes and, finally, a measure to get the proportions right. He loaded the complete kit into a bag, took it to the car and drove off.

* * *

He recalled the first time he'd met Eric Best – it was over two years ago now. The landlord of the Huntsman had dialled 999, reporting fighting on the premises. Thomas was only around the corner when the call came over the pocket set, so was first to arrive on the scene at what would have been the final attack.

Best was lying on his back defenceless and already showing evidence of having received a hammering, with an eye half-closed and blood pouring from his swollen mouth. Kneeling astride him and looking every bit the aggressor was his attacker, a nasty piece of work, greasy haired, wearing jeans and a black sleeveless T-shirt, displaying his tattoos. His arm was raised, holding a jagged, broken bottle, its vicious edges poised to be pushed and turned into Eric's face to cause an injury that would probably blind or at least make a facial laceration that would sicken a nurse.

Pushing his way through a gawking, non-committal audience of customers, regardless of his own safety, Thomas cannoned into the attacker just as the bottle commenced its downward journey, sending him violently off-balance, the bottle involuntarily being thrown clear of Eric and colliding with a harmless clink against the legs of a stool.

Seeing the uniform and realising that he was being grabbed by a no-nonsense policeman, the man made no effort to retrieve the bottle or pursue his attack.

Instead, to Thomas's relief, who didn't fancy being bottled either, he had resigned to surrender.

Thomas was getting to his feet as his back-up support appeared and, with four policemen now on the premises, the prisoner was handcuffed and conveyed to the police station cells.

Eric had reluctantly agreed to be taken by ambulance to casualty for attention with a suspected concussion from a head butt and a split and torn mouth which required painful stitching.

Statements had been taken from the landlord and an elderly customer and, the following day, Thomas, updated with the events which had taken place in the bar prior to his arrival, had visited the stables, in those days a small establishment and Eric's first, known as Firfettle Farm.

Accepting the fact that Eric had not thrown a punch in retaliation or even said anything to provoke an attack, he was interested to know what had been the motive for the assault. Eric was grateful that Thomas had saved his sandy-haired, freckled looks from being suitable for the viewing of over eighteens only and, when Thomas arrived to complete his enquiries, he had greeted him warmly. The policeman was satisfied by the explanation of events put forward in distorted words through Eric's swollen lips.

With only a week to the Cheltenham National Hunt Festival, Eric, who ran both a straight and very successful yard, had sacked his amateur jockey that previous day for riding his second race for the benefit of a gambling syndicate rather than the stable, taking the necessary action before the stewards had picked up on the abnormalities of the result. The attacker, who was a stranger to Eric until the assault, happened to be a brother of the sacked jockey, Billy Jefferson, and a member of the syndicate.

After making the statement, Eric had shown Thomas around his stables, proudly introducing him to some of the famous names which had been repeatedly heading the racing results. Admitting to his little knowledge of horses, it had come out in conversation that Thomas sculpted, and Eric, who had been trying to think of a way to reward him for his heroics without seeming insulting, seized on the opportunity to arrange an introduction with an owner who had wanted a bronze of one of his horses which had been tragically killed.

With the use of the owner's video recordings and mountains of photographs, Thomas was able to create a remarkable likeness – to the surprise of Eric and the great pleasure of the owner. From then on, with sincerity rather than charity, Eric had put a few commissions Thomas's way and that had been the start of their friendship.

* * *

Forty minutes later Thomas turned off the main road and into the country lane leading to the stables and arrived at Eagle Lodge, pulling his car, an MGB, to a stop in the paddock yard. It was 10am and a warm day. The sun was bright, its light throwing hard contrasts and projecting the dimensions of the buildings. How he wished he were able to paint as well as sculpt. He took his kit out of the car and shut the door. It broke the silence of the yard. Yet to his surprise nobody appeared except Meg, Eric's sheepdog bitch who snaked up to every visitor with a grin often mistaken for a snarl. She offered her back to be scratched. Thomas obliged, while waiting for someone to appear, but no one did. Instead the telephone bell rudely broke the slumbering silence and rang persistently, eventually stopping with indignant abruptness, confirming the absence of any other human being.

A scan around the yard suggested that a string of horses was still out on morning exercise. Some of the boxes were open – beds slept in but residents temporarily absent.

Thomas removed his kit, left it on the car bonnet and, crossing the huge well-manicured lawn of the courtyard, took a leisurely stroll around the boxes along its perimeter with Meg bouncing happily ahead of him. Three fillies hung their heads out in neighbourly congregation, interested but unperturbed by his presence. Thomas raised his hand fondly to the grey Blue Dolphin. She nuzzled it but kept an eye on Meg. Blue Dolphin had been his last commission and with a dished, Arab-type head, she'd been a horse he'd enjoyed sculpting.

Eyecatcher's box was empty so, remembering what Summer had told him, he looked around for the horse's new secure quarters, expecting to activate alarms at any minute. But after looking into thirty-four boxes he still hadn't found Eyecatcher.

He looked at his watch and saw that he'd been there twenty minutes. That suddenly made him feel frustrated. He wanted to get started. He walked across to the house to double check if anyone was about. As he crossed the yard towards the side of the house, he caught a glimpse of two other boxes next door to Eric's offices and situated in front of the all-weather, indoor school fifty yards beyond. He approached them and, to him, they appeared empty, the door of one swinging squeakily like a saloon door after the Sheriff had walked in. The other was closed on the bottom but the top half looked like a frame waiting for a picture to be put in it. As Thomas got closer nothing appeared to alter his conclusions except that he now noticed the half-closed box had a camera trained on it which was silently watching from an elevated position at the corner of the house.

That must be where Eyecatcher's been moved to, he thought, now feeling a bit uneasy for, although he was doing nothing wrong, the cameras made him feel that he shouldn't be there – it would look like he was snooping. He reached the stable door, looked up to the camera – it appeared inactive. Expecting the box to be empty, he popped his head over the top of the door to look in but, as he did, he jerked back with sudden fright as a bantam took flight out of the stable and into his face. As Thomas realised what it was he regained his composure and saw the unmistakable Eyecatcher, unguarded and picking at his hay. He looked up at Thomas, unconcerned and continued to pick and chew. Now able to carry on, Thomas returned to the car for his clay and tools. He passed the fillies, heads held high in unison as they looked across to the distant road. One whinnied loudly and Thomas heard the many clip-clops of approaching horses' hooves. The string was returning. As they entered the paddock yard, Meg took up her place on the lawn and lay down, tail thumping the ground.

"Morning Thomas," Eric called from the rear of

the string, touching his cap out of habit with his crop as he passed. “Be with you in a minute – just got to sort the rabble out.” Eric dismounted, handing his lead to one of the lads and rushed amongst the others like a cavalry sergeant handing out orders and instructions. Each charge was led to its respective box and the stables filled, the yard a hive of activity as the lads unsaddled, brushed down and watered their horses. Thomas looked out for Summer but couldn’t see her anywhere.

“If you’re looking for Summer,” Eric said, reading his mind, “she’s slipped into town to get the horse box plated.”

“Yeh, I was wondering where she was. Did she mention the sculpture to you?” Thomas asked.

“No, to be quite honest with you. I’ve been so busy every day, I haven’t seen much of her at all this week. Eyecatcher’s up this way,” he said indicating with his eyes towards the all-weather school. “Come on, I’ll show you.”

“I’ll just get my stuff from the car,” Thomas said and quickly picked it up from the bonnet, hurrying to catch up with the quickly stepping trainer.

Eric opened the stable door and greeted Eyecatcher with fondness. He unbuckled and stripped back his blanket, displaying him with pride. The horse’s coat was as shiny as Thomas’s boots had been that morning before court.

“Christ, he’s looking well,” Thomas said in admiration.

“Isn’t he just,”Eric beamed. “Plenty of muscle there to put in your sculpture, Thomas. Well, I’ll leave him with you, I’ve got work to do. Give you a shout at about what – one o'clock? We'll go to the pub for a glass and a sandwich."

"OK, fine," said Thomas, happy enough to be left alone with his subject. "Nothing I should know about these cameras is there?" now noticing another one inside the stable.

"Those? No, don't worry, that's all switched off. See you later."

At one o'clock Thomas was still struggling with the armature, the pattern which was to be the core of his sculpture, knowing it to be fruitless to go further until he had the basic structure correct.

"How's it shaping?" Eric asked, sticking his head over the door.

"Difficult as usual but I think I've got him."

Eric looked at the taped and bandaged wire stick-horse Thomas was holding. He wasn't very impressed but, then, he never was until he saw the finished article, unable to appreciate the importance of this crucial stage.

"Right, that's it," Thomas said, carefully putting down the armature. "Come on, I could murder a pint." Thomas cleared his stuff out of the stable, making sure nothing was left that could harm Eye-catcher and delicately carried the result of his morning's work to the MGB, placing it on the passenger seat.

"Jump in the Range Rover," offered Eric as Thomas closed the passenger door.

"No, it's alright, I'll follow you down in my car, thanks. Save me coming back later."

"As you like," replied Eric, window down and starting off.

In five minutes they arrived at the Rose and

Crown. Eric introduced him to the select few people in the bar, called the round and ordered the sandwiches.

"Beef all right, Thomas?" he asked.

"Fine," said Thomas, now hungry. He looked across the bar counter into the lounge opposite and saw that it was packed to capacity.

"It's busy in there," Thomas said.

"Always is lunchtimes," Eric replied. "That's why I come into the bar. Come on, let's sit down."

They sat at a table away from the door and window. Thomas downed half his pint in one go. Eric just took two mouthfuls of his half, fearing that drinking too liberally at lunchtime would make him sleepy in the afternoon.

"I needed that," Thomas said, putting his glass down.

"Hey, what's the idea of moving Eyecatcher into a box with a camera," he asked, fishing for a comment about the death threats. "Getting him used to being a film star when he retires or what?"

He noticed a slight blush of uneasiness on Eric's face.

"Oh, that's just Mr Corran's idea. As I said, don't worry about it," he replied trying to brush it off.

"Well, is he afraid that the horse is going to get nobbled or what?" Thomas pressed.

"Well, you can't be too careful."

"But you've never bothered before," Thomas continued. "Has something happened or what? Anything I can help with?" He didn't want to show that Summer had told him anything.

"No," Eric said convincingly. "I'm sure Mr Corran has no need for the police."

"Should I ask him?" asked Thomas still not happy.

"If the man says 'no', then it's 'no', OK, Thomas?" Eric said firmly, leaving him in no doubt that he didn't want to discuss the matter any further. Eric never did talk easily about his owners' business and this was no exception. Thomas drank down the rest of his pint and broke the pregnant pause by suggesting another round.

"Same again?"

"No, not for me," said Eric, holding on to his glass which was still nearly full.

While Thomas was at the bar he considered what Eric had said. Something wasn't right. He was too touchy for one thing and there was something false about the cameras. In spite of them, security at the stables was non-existent. He decided to leave it there, determined not to spoil the day. Returning to the table he said, "Are you confident about the Arc?"

"No, I'm not," Eric replied, worried. "The bookies have got him as an odds-on certainty and that puts the pressure on me. He travelled very badly last year, had a touch of colic. It was touch and go if he'd run or not but Mr Corran had so much money on him antepost I had no choice but to get him to the start. I tell you, no other horse would have done it for me. Do you know, he'd been catching up on his sleep all that morning – too tired to eat. He's incredible. But this is his last race. If he wins this, he retires undefeated."

"An awful shame if he is beaten," Thomas said.

"Don't talk about it," Eric answered, afraid of the thought.

Thomas wanted to ask if Corran had bet heavily

on the horse antepost this time but thought better of it, not wanting to sound as if he was prying. Two plates of beef sandwiches were put on the table, quickly followed by salt and mustard. They both tucked in. Thomas noticed Eric's hand shaking as he held the sandwich. For someone far short of middle age, his face looked very drawn and lined, a condition which could have been accelerated by the pressures of success but he seemed to have a nervousness about him, a pre-occupation that Thomas hadn't seen before. Perhaps it was just as well that this was Eyecatcher's last race. Any death-threats after that wouldn't be Eric's worry.

"Will you be doing any more of your sculpture this afternoon?"

"No," replied Thomas, "I'll take that home now as a basis to start from. Alright if I call and see him again to do a bit more in a day or two?"

"Sure," Eric said, "Help yourself, you're alright for a week or so but don't leave it too close to the race."

"Fine," Thomas said.

Eric looked at his watch and stood up.

"Sorry to leave you but I've got to get back. I'm meeting new owners at 2.30."

Thomas got up, apologising. "Sorry, why didn't you tell me earlier."

"That's OK chum, no panic," he said as they left the pub together and walked to the cars.

"Thanks Eric, I'll give you a ring."

"Yes, do that. Oh, and put a pound on Sparrow Hawk in the four o'clock tomorrow. No, make that a pound each way." Thomas waved and drove off.

On the way home he felt uneasy about Eric's

attitude in the Rose and Crown. If he had been worried over the safety of the horse why hadn't he confided in him, and there again, why was the security non-existent at the stables that morning? Where had the new French lad been? If he was supposed to double-up as a guard for the horse, then he must have been hiding in the hay rack or somewhere because Thomas hadn't seen him. Eric was covering up for Corran and it was going against his style. Something was up, things just didn't add up.

As Thomas walked up his front path, he heard his telephone ringing. With hands full, he struggled to balance everything while he searched through his pockets to find his key. Opening the door, he put his things on the floor and picked up the receiver. It was Summer.

"Hi," she said. "Aren't you friends with me, lover?"

"Course," he said. "Why?"

"Well, you drove past me, nose in the air just now as I was coming back to the yard."

"Sorry, love," Thomas said, not realising he had used the word 'love'. "I was miles away."

"As usual," she said. "How's the sculpture getting on anyway?"

"Give me a chance," he said, "I only started it this morning, but so far so good. Hey, do you fancy the pictures tomorrow night and a few drinks after?"

"Yes, why not – be a nice change," she said. "Not too late a night though, promise?"

"Promise," he said.

"I'll arrange baby-sitters," Summer said with enthusiasm. "Pick me up at seven. I'll be ready."

"OK, see you and may the force be with you."

She laughed at the adaptation and put the phone down with a giggle.

Thomas spent the evening in his shed, getting down to some serious work on his sculpture. Taking stronger steel than that he'd used in the morning, he cut, bent, angled and re-bent until he had an exact match to the armature he'd made in the morning. Then he went outside and welded all the pieces together to form a rigid frame which he could build on. He then wrapped this with wire and mesh, more so in the bulky rib and neck areas, so that the clay would have something to key on to. Finally he compared it with Summer's photographs and made alterations until it was perfect. He fixed the finished structure to a stand and began to apply the clay, a very fine-fibred porcelain which would allow for a detailed finish, suitable for bronze casting. As soon as the basic shape of the horse appeared, Thomas stopped working and covered his sculpture with a damp cloth to prevent the clay from hardening. Having done enough for one day, he went to bed, pleased with his progress and satisfied the bronze would be ready in time for the big race.

CHAPTER FIVE

Summer telephoned him at 10 the next morning.

"Hi, can't talk for long," she said, a little breathless. "I'm in the middle of mucking out. Thachit Corran is running a buffet dance at the New Ritz in Gordonstow next Thursday to toast Eyecatcher and wish him bon voyage for the Arc."

"A bit premature, isn't it?" Thomas queried.

"Who cares?" Summer said flippantly, "as long as it's free. He'll probably be having another one before the race, knowing him. Anyway all staff and friends are invited, so I'm asking you. Fancy it? Sorry to spring it on you at such short notice but they want the acceptances in straight away."

"Yeah, sounds great. Put me down," he replied enthusiastically. "It'll be interesting if nothing else. I've never seen Corran in the flesh and only caught the odd glimpse of him on the TV on race coverages."

"You've missed nothing," she remarked hurriedly. "OK, I'll see you tonight. Bye, must fly. Oh, one other thing – it's formal dress. You know, black tie. See you."

Replacing the receiver, Thomas wondered if his dinner suit would still fit him. He searched it out of the wardrobe to check. Trying it on, he was relieved to see it did but, bare chested and without the white shirt and bow tie, he hardly looked like James Bond. He put the suit aside and went back to work on his sculpture. Removing the damp cloth, he stood back and judged what he had done so far. Rough as it was, he was still happy with its progress and eagerly continued, refining it with each addition of clay.

Three hours later he put down his tools, washed his hands and made himself a coffee. Thinking of Thatchit Corran, he tried to picture the man who would produce make-up for gay men. In hindsight, Thomas accepted that he had knowingly mixed with one or two gays in his time. Some had been in his circle of friends when he was a student at polytechnic long before he had aspirations to be a policeman. He found the effeminate ways of the more obvious ones amusing. He was always intrigued by the way they seemed to pull the birds, probably due to their chattyness, he thought, rather than sexual prowess. But a man who produced make-up for them he couldn't imagine.

At seven o'clock outside Summer's house, Thomas gave a toot on his horn. She opened the door, ready and a little out of breath. Although her son was fourteen, Summer would make sure he had company if she was going out. Kissing him good-night and leaving last minute instructions for the sitters to help themselves, satisfied that there was no more to be done, she jumped into the car next to Thomas and sighed.

"I thought I'd never be ready on time. Only just got back from Nottingham. We had a winner at fourteen to one."

"What was it called?" Thomas asked, half

screwing up his face, afraid to hear the reply as he started the engine and pulled away.

"Sparrow Hawk."

"Shit!" exclaimed Thomas.

"Pardon?" Summer said, bemused and rather surprised at his reaction.

"Balls! Eric told me to back that and I clean forgot about it."

"You must be in love," she joked.

"Did it win by much?" he asked and then "No – I don't want to know."

"Eight lengths," she answered, turning the screw.

He looked at her sparkling eyes and broke into a smile.

They weren't long getting to the cinema but parking proved to be a problem. After about five minutes he finally found a space. Summer made a check of her appearance in the mirror.

"Mmm, you smell nice," he said.

"Thanks," she said kissing him on the nose. "It's Beautiful."

"I haven't smelt that on you before," Thomas said, his nose now teasing her behind her ear. Enjoying the fun, she pushed him away.

"Get orf! Does it have that effect on you? I don't know, first Eyecatcher, now you!"

"Eyecatcher! What's he got to do with it?"

"This perfume. I couldn't wear it when I was looking after him. He gets as randy as hell."

"And you can't push a horse off!" he laughed.

"You're crude sometimes," she remarked, getting out of the car.

"I'm crude!" he said, "It was your story."

She was still smiling. "What film are you taking

me to see?" she asked, threading her arm through his and leaning on his shoulder.

"I don't know what's on," he said.

"Nor me," she replied, "but I don't mind what we see as long as you don't go to sleep."

"Who, me?" he said, trying to sound surprised.

"Yes, you!"

The evening was warm enough for shirtsleeves but with that close stillness that promised thunder. They queued for Steven Spielberg's latest. Not wanting his voice to carry, Thomas discreetly said, "That security you were telling me about was non-existent. A couple of switched-off cameras and that's about it."

"You're telling me," she said, "and all that fuss to replace me with a man because of the threats, and then he's never there. It's Eric who has to do the horse. I mean, I still could but he won't allow me to – says it's not fair until after the danger's over. I ask you, what danger? I think it's just a hoax."

"Ravir's never there?" Thomas said, "How do you mean, he's never there?"

"Well, he's got hold of this white Porsche from somewhere and goes out in it after breakfast. Then we don't see him for the rest of the day."

"What does Eric say about it?"

"Nothing, and it's not our place to make comment, but, by the way this Ravir behaves, you'd swear that he was running the show. Do you know he's even got a medalion with his initials in diamonds. He's more like an owner than a stable lad. They must pay them bloody well in France or he's landed some hefty betting coups!"

Thomas couldn't concentrate on the film, turning

things over in his mind, considering what Summer had told him and trying to permutate it with the other facts. The threats – if there were threats – could be coming from one of Corran's culture producers. There was the make-up, the Arc, the cameras and now a stable lad with a Porsche. He juggled them all around but they refused to fall into any reasonable explanation.

Summer was deep into the film, only occasionally glancing at Thomas to check that he hadn't nodded off.

"Fancy a nightcap?" Thomas suggested on the way out "The Arc Haven Hotel is just round the corner."

"OK, so long as it is only the one. I promised Dave and Jan I wouldn't be late home. It's not easy to get baby-sitters at short notice."

The bar of the Arc Haven was heaving and Thomas had snapped out of his thoughts.

"White wine for me," Summer shouted above the din, the jukebox blasting out Michael Jackson.

He struggled to the front and fought to get served. To save queuing for a second, he bought two bottles of beer and two glasses of wine, aware that Summer had only agreed to the one, and endeavoured to try to find her without spilling a drop. Seeing Thomas precariously carrying the bottles and glasses, she moved towards him but instead of taking the glasses from him, Summer undid the zip of his trousers. Before she could do anything else, he turned in a panic and found a window sill on which to set the beer and glasses down safely. She was still giggling as, very embarrassed, he did up his flies.

"I owe you one for that," he said, now in a

position to appreciate the joke. On the wall near them, a poster for a forthcoming 'Miss Wet T-shirt' contest caught his eye.

"Wouldn't mind seeing that," Thomas said lecherously.

"Oh, you would?" Summer replied. "It's not fair. They never have wet jock strap competitions or wet tight white pants. Ooh, I'd go for that! Men in tight white pants." She went for his zip again. This time he backed away just in time.

"Spoilsport," she said.

At that moment Summer saw Pamela Corran come into the bar followed by the French stable lad, Serge Ravir. She nudged Thomas to look across, as Pamela and her latest escort came in and, seeing there was little room, turned and left, without noticing Summer or Thomas.

"Well, well, well," Summer said in bitchy admiration. "She doesn't waste much time. That was Mr Ravir."

Thomas had not realised who it was, and had only caught a glimpse of him. Short, dark and, Thomas supposed, handsome. He felt jealous but made no comment. After all he had a beautiful woman with him as well.

CHAPTER SIX

Early the following Monday morning Thomas summoned up all his energy in an effort to merely sit up in bed. The alarm clock had obeyed its instructions and this was the first stage in his personal promise to get up before sunrise. But second thoughts became twenty second thoughts before he could decide on taking the next stage – splash his eyes with cold water. Then, he dressed warmly in thick pullover, two pairs of trousers and a sheepskin coat, and sat to drink an orange juice, hoping it would transfuse into him some of its freshness, while he considered whether or not to negotiate the final stage – open the door and step out into the remains of the night, which had been his purposeful plan before going to bed. Now, eyes still squinting in the artificial light, the warmth of his clothing coaxed him back to sleep; but only for a brief shallow snooze. The clink of the milkman's bottles opened his eyes, reminding him there was human life outside despite the alien hour.

Only slightly encouraged by this, he heaved himself up, switched off the light and did it! He slammed the door behind him with final decision.

Driving to the gallops, Thomas had already witnessed two sunrises as he reached the crest of two hills in succession before following the road leading to the stretch. Instead of enjoying this rare experience, he only saw it as a double reminder of how early he had got up. Eric had booked Eyecatcher in for an early morning exercise before the pre-breakfast rush of the other stables and Thomas was taking the opportunity of joining the select group to see the great horse in action. The photographs were serving their purpose, but he needed to see the horse again to get the feel of him and bring his sculpture to life.

Seeing Eric's Range Rover, he parked next to it and sat watching in awe as Eyecatcher went through his paces, pulverising the opposition, with his head turned comically down and to the side. Spotting the trainer, Thomas got out and joined him. Eric was standing with an air of pride. They were watching poetry in motion and Thomas had often thought that in the world of engineering this horse's sire and dam would have been the holders of designer awards. God, I hope I can do him justice, he thought to himself.

"How's the sculpture coming along?" Eric asked, "Can I see it?"

"Of course. Come to the car and I'll show you."

Eric walked to the car with him and Thomas carefully removed his Eyecatcher.

"Hey, that's a bloody big improvement from the last time I saw it. Not bad at all."

"Mr Corran isn't about is he?" Thomas checked, "I wouldn't like to let the cat out of the bag."

"No, he's in France on business – not due back

until this Thursday,"Eric said reassuringly. "Are you coming to the do with Summer?"

"Hope to if duty permits," Thomas replied.

"Good. I must say it really is shaping up," said Eric, admiring the sculpture again. "You want to show it to the television people?"

"No fear," said Thomas, looking a little startled. He had noticed the camera crew was active. It was a common occurrence before any big race to have a build-up with interviews and rundowns on the main contenders – weighing up their chances and, on top of that, Eyecatcher was the housewife's favourite, the public idol. You didn't have to be a racing fan to know of him. Like many superstars, his personality had projected him beyond the sport, promoting him into a celebrity, but Thomas didn't want to be drawn into any feature by way of his sculpture. Not only did he prefer to remain in the shadows when it came to work outside the police force but, besides that, exposure at this stage would blow the birthday surprise.

"I'll get this lot away," he said hurriedly, "before they come over to interview you."

Eric laughed, "Chicken!" as Thomas started the car and backed away over the grass just as the trainer was being surrounded by the media men, swamped out of sight. There was no point in waving.

Thomas turned and carefully drove back against the flow of traffic – thoroughbreds which were trotting up the track in their stable strings like open necklaces, each pearl with the price tag of a diamond.

Content with having seen the points he needed to work on, his senses had now caught up with his body and he was enjoying the experience of the morning.

That undefinable smell of Autumn's arrival was in his nostrils, the sky was a high blue and he felt like eating a cooked breakfast. He reflected that on a nice day a life amongst horses had its good points, but that first hour of waking in the darkness would make sure he'd never get hooked on it.

CHAPTER SEVEN

Thursday came around very quickly. With Richard on leave, Thomas had to share the burden of the extra work-load. Richard had tried to clear his tray but had asked Thomas to do one or two favours for him in his absence. One of these was to chase up a doctor's statement describing the injuries in one of Richard's assault cases. The statement was two weeks overdue and holding up the file. Failing again to see the doctor, and leaving yet another message at the hospital, Thomas decided he'd give the cardboard pasties and pies on offer at the police station canteen a miss for his dinner. These were a standing dish all through the week. He hadn't looked at what variations were on the menu but he wanted a salad, and these would already have been taken by the figure-conscious office girls.

Passing the Chinese take-away he considered it less of a risk putting his stomach on the line with them rather than the canteen. He looked in. Good, it was empty, except for a drunk. Mrs Chai was behind the counter, watching the television, set high for customers' benefit, as he entered.

"Lo," she said to Thomas.

"Hello, Mrs Chai," Thomas replied. "I'll have a

chicken Chinese-style please." She scribbled a number on her pad and swivelling on her stool stuffed the order sheet through the hatch. Thomas had ordered assuming that the drunk who sat at the counter trying to focus on the menu, would be a long time. He was trying to pick it up off the counter, not having realised that it was under glass.

"You busy today?" asked Mrs Chai.

"No, I'm not busy," replied Thomas.

"Ah, you good boy," she said, "You no busy good. Me no busy no good."

Thomas waited for his brain to register what she had said and laughed. There was a lot to be said for these Chinese proverbs. Before he could get into further conversation, the dinner-time rush entered the little take-away. He stood about awkwardly waiting for his order. Thomas was wearing a cape, convenient for smuggling meals through the streets without being seen. Money in hand, he was now standing at the back next to the window, checking that the road leading to the station was clear of senior officers and ready for a quick getaway. He heard Mrs Chai shout 'Ticken Chinese Style', and stepped forward to give her a five pound note and take the carrier containing his order. The meal was marked up as £2.40, but before he could reach her she shouted, "For you, only one pound."

The entire crowd turned round in unison and looked at him before checking the menu price of Chicken Chinese Style. He felt himself blush and accepted the meal, paying the pound.

"God," he thought, "I wish she wouldn't do that." Thomas left the take-away like an anonymous phantom.

With his mind on the evening ahead, the remainder of the afternoon dragged like one of those times when the clock seemed to take more than eight hours to go through a shift. He asked his duty sergeant for an hour off so that he wouldn't have to rush to get ready for the New Ritz.

At 7.30pm, the taxi Summer had ordered for them was waiting outside. Thomas had been ready for some time, surprisingly having had a first-time success at putting on his new leather bow tie – he'd never been able to master his conventional velvet one. He coolly walked out towards the taxi. Summer was already on board and, seating himself in the back next to her, he was pleasantly startled by her hair style. There was so much of it, a backdrop wider than her shoulders. It was both very full and curled, not merely bubbly but frothy, giving her a sexy, new look.

"That's a beautiful way you've done your hair," he complimented. "What are you doing down there?" She had slid down the seat, almost sitting on the taxi floor.

"I didn't want to get you into any trouble with Cath," Summer answered.

"You're daft sometimes," he said and, smiling, made to give a friendly ruffle to her hair.

"You dare," she warned. "It took me nearly an hour and a half to get it like this."

"Sorry," he said and kissed her instead. She pulled him down and whispered, "I've never had it in the back of a taxi."

He sat up, straightened his bow tie and winked. She winked back and they both laughed but, as the taxi drew up outside the New Ritz shortly after, it remained Summer's ambition.

Entering the foyer, Summer left Thomas in order to check her appearance in the ladies' room. As he watched her walk away he found the overall impression of her stunning. He felt impatient. He wished he had fulfilled her ambition in the taxi, he wanted to bed her now. A greeting from behind stopped him from following her.

"PC Cord. What are you doing here?"

He turned to see his Divisional Chief Superintendent and a solicitor, Graham Kirby, with whom he was on Christian name terms. They were with female company.

"Thomas, what are you having to drink?" Graham enquired.

"Not for me, not yet," Thomas said, slightly raising his hand. "I've only just come in."

"Sorry sir," Thomas turned to his Chief Super. "You were saying."

"That's alright lad. I was just wondering how you found your way in here."

Unaware that he was sparing Thomas the embarrassment of having to explain, the Chief Superintendent didn't wait for a reply but introduced him to his wife and to Graham's regular escort, whom Thomas had met before. After the briefest of courteous remarks, the Chief Superintendent and his wife excused themselves and with their friends, headed for the bar, just missing Summer as she reappeared.

Summer and Thomas decided to give the bar a miss and go straight to the function room. It was already occupied with what Thomas estimated to be at least two hundred guests and his immediate priority was to find their designated table, one of the many around the dance floor. Summer found it near a pillar away from direct ear-shot of the stage speakers.

"What would you like to drink?" Thomas asked, ready to get started.

"Don't worry. Sit down," Summer told him, "It's all free tonight, waiter service only."

Now Thomas understood the significance of the early reply to the invitation and the reason why the Chief Superintendent was there – he and Graham, who were close friends, never missed out on a free do, provided it was above board. Thomas wondered if the Chief Superintendent was aware of the investigation going on into Smudge and whether or not it was prudent that he had come. As a police constable, he considered himself small fry but, looking around he recognised several faces, respected public figures amongst them, who – if they weren't careful towards the latter part of the night – were going to have their guard dangerously low due to the free drinks.

No sooner had Thomas sat down than a waiter asked him for his order. He'd start with a pint of beer – which didn't meet with much approval. Summer went silly and ordered a Harvey Wallbanger. Thomas smiled. Here we go, he thought, his eyes wandering to adjoining tables. He saw that it was lethal to empty your glass, for as soon as you did the drink was replenished whether ordered or not. The only way to hold things up seemed to be to change the order.

At 8.30 huge trolleys laden with salads, smoked salmon, fresh salmon, sliced beef and game pie were wheeled into the areas behind the tables. A Toast Master dressed in the full regalia banged his gavel and announced to a hushed audience, "My Lords, honoured guests, ladies and gentlemen, the buffet is served."

Thomas and Summer rose, joined the others and helped themselves. The free drink was certainly beginning to take effect. Everybody was chatty and good humoured. Thomas filled his plate to capacity and felt a bit guilty but nobody noticed. In fact, people were going back for more.

"Which one is Corran?" Thomas asked, looking around as they ate their food.

"He's not here – probably upstairs." She was having to shout over the noise of the disco which had started.

"Why, what's upstairs?" Thomas shouted back.

"A press conference, I should think. Eric will be there, a few racing celebrities, jockeys and no doubt a pop star or film star. Don't forget, the main purpose for the do is to promote Eyecatcher. The horse is just an excuse, a reason to invite people."

Thomas looked around him again and thought whether the French farmers were paying for it all or if Smudge was a separate account.

"Fancy a dance?" Thomas said.

"Sure," said Summer, knocking back her fourth Harvey Wallbanger.

At the end of the record, the music stopped and the Toast Master interrupted again. The two tiptoed back to their table.

"My Lords, honoured guests, ladies and gentlemen. Please be upstanding for your host. Thatchit Corran, Esquire! Sir!"

Everybody rose to their feet and started applauding. Thomas reluctantly joined in. God knows why I'm doing this, he thought, but he considered it less conspicuous than to be nonconforming. Thatchit Corran, with what appeared to be an entourage of heavily made-up gay transvestites, walked down the centre of the floor and onto the stage. Thomas relaxed as he realized that they were the group hired to provide live music for the evening and not Corran's hareem.

Corran himself was now standing at the microphone, and Thomas took an instant dislike to him. He was the type of man who wouldn't have class no matter how much he spent trying to obtain it. He was a big man, about six feet but overweight. The most striking feature of all was his silly, coloured blond hair. It was obviously not his natural colour if the ginger Mexican moustache was anything to go by, and it was pathetically styled, collar length and wavey, exaggerating his receding hair line. He might have got away with it had he been a cavalier or musketeer of days long past, but even they would have been suspicious of the synthetic colour. Thomas remembered it being mentioned that Pamela was looking for bigger premises to expand her hairdressing business. If this was an example of her talents then 'Curled up and Died' would be an apt name for her new salon. He thought how stupid the man would look if he were to wear any of the hats traditional in the racing scene.

However, Thatchit Corran didn't strike Thomas as being a gender-bender himself. Oh, he was bent alright, but not in that way. No, Corran seemed to be attempting to find a softer image for his features –

which would have been more at home under a bald head – and wasn't having much success. Nevertheless, Thomas didn't like him. He reminded him of the type of bullying shop floor factory worker that management would promote to use as a troubleshooter, more for brawn rather than brains. Thomas had identified them during his twelve months work-experience in the car industry before he abandoned it to apply in England to become a policeman where vacancies were more abundant than in his home Welsh force. It said something for the police in general that they had no call for their sort.

Helped again by the Toast Master, Corran asked for glasses to be raised in a toast to Eyecatcher, and as 'Bon Voyage' was added, Thomas concluded that this was directed to the horse and not the cosmetics. They toasted Eyecatcher with champagne, which must have been provided when Summer and Thomas were dancing. Before the next toast, Thomas took the opportunity to sneak out to the loo, conveniently avoiding the speeches and mutual back-patting which was to follow.

"I'll be back in two shakes of a lamb's tail," he whispered to Summer.

"Stop bragging!" she said.

He returned fifteen minutes later, timing his re-entry just as Eric was leaving the stage.

"Where did you get to?" Summer asked.

"I went up to the private room for a nose – thought Ravir might have been there. I haven't seen him tonight. Have you?"

"No," said Summer "but if he is who he says he is then he should be doing his job back at Eagle Lodge.

If ever there was an opportunity to get to Eyecatcher then this would be it."

Thomas agreed with her but, before being able to say so, the Royal toast was being proposed. Down went the last of the champagne and Summer was well on the way, giggling girlishly and looking for a refill from Thomas's glass.

The group, with a very professional sound in spite of their looks, opened with their current hit and Summer grabbed Thomas's hand, pulling him up to dance. As they gyrated Thomas's eyes wandered across to the top table where Corran was standing, introducing his daughter to all and sundry. Thomas noticed that even her father couldn't resist giving her a friendly slap on the rump, yet it didn't cheer her up. She looked totally bored. Cameras started flashing as Thatchit Corran mingled and posed with the well-known, upstanding members of the party and it was at this point Thomas noticed the Chief Superintendent and his wife sensibly move from their host's immediate vicinity.

Back at their table, Summer saw Pamela for the first time.

"Pamela's over there," she said to Thomas. "You should dance with her – after all, she's given you a good commission."

He didn't really want to and felt a bit bashful after her stand-offish attitude over the telephone, but he mustered enough courage to go over and ask her.

"You're sure you won't mind," he checked with Summer.

"You're coming back I hope," she joked.

"Eventually," he teased. She poked her tongue out at him, but was still smiling.

He walked up to Pamela, expecting to be refused. She looked as if she had been poured into her dress. It was black, shimmering and ankle length, the back bare and scooped right down to – 'Christ, what an arse!' "Dance?" he said.

"Yes, why should I always ask," she replied and he was astonished to see her smile. 'I'll have to wear this suit more often,' he thought.

Dancing in that dress was damn nigh impossible for her so, being the gentleman he was, Thomas held her hips and slowed down the tempo.

"Does your father have his hair cut by you?" he asked.

"I have done it once or twice but he had it rinsed and waved in France this week. It's horrific. I'm ashamed to be seen with him."

Thomas agreed but decided not to say so. He reflected that he'd have to think of a better name for her salon. She put her arms around his neck and came in close. Now he was on dangerous ground. He moved with the music so that he could position himself to see if Summer was looking but he couldn't see her. Hell, he thought, I hope she doesn't think I'm doing this, but it got worse. Pamela had now positioned her crotch onto the front of his thigh and was definitely pressing herself into him. It was having an effect.

"God, if they play this another three times," he whispered, "it could be my favourite record."

She laughed. She actually laughed! With that, a searing pain stung his behind. Summer had just pinched it. He turned around to see her twirling away with her partner. Back down to earth, he saw the dance out, thanked Pamela and walked across to Summer.

"Thought you needed help," she said.

"Yeah, I suppose I did," he replied. "Thanks." Without exchanging another word, they began to dance. Summer latched herself to the same leg in the same manner as Pamela had, only Summer was better at it. Her brilliant white dress was split to her thigh and that was pretty high seeing that her legs gave the illusion of going right up to her armpits.

"Carry on like this and I'll be wearing this suit to bed," he said. An approving purr in his ear was the only reply. By the end of the dance, Thomas was experiencing difficulty in walking. His tight trousers were getting tighter.

Thatchit Corran approached across the dance floor. Thomas had noticed him leering at Summer for some time.

"Summer," he said loudly, full of his own self-importance, as if he hadn't seen her for years, "You are looking ravishing. May I have this dance?" He completely ignored Thomas, who didn't give Summer a chance to reply. He lifted her up and turned to Corran.

"Sorry mate, I've just stepped on her foot. Try again later."

He carried a speechless, euphoric Summer out of the hotel and into the street. The dirty, slobbering sod – it was bad enough that Corran was going to get his hands on his sculpture. He wasn't going to put them on his woman as well.

Summer gave him a long lingering kiss before he put her down.

"Let's walk home," she suggested. "It's not cold."

By the time they had reached the end of the street, the fresh air had reacted with Summer's alcohol intake and she was flat out. Thomas ended up calling a taxi, carrying her into her house and putting her to bed, a frustrated man.

* * *

At 10.20 the following morning, the Divisional Chief Superintendent picked up his telephone and dialled twenty-eight, the internal number for the fraud squad office. Detective Constable Reynolds answered.

"Fraud."

"Who speaks?" the Chief Super asked. Reynolds, immediately recognising his voice, answered with careful respect.

"DC Reynolds, Sir."

"Is your Inspector there, son?" the senior officer enquired.

"No, he's with crime intelligence picking up some photocopies, Sir, I believe. Shall I fetch him?"

"No, just tell him to ring me when he returns."

"Yes Sir," Reynolds replied, but the telephone was already dead. The receiver was still in the DC's hand when the Inspector walked in with the photocopies under his arm. Alex McGuire was a red-haired Scotsman, totally predictable and a good boss who spoke his mind. But his impatience was a source of amusement to the squad, an impatience which belied his academic qualifications, holding him back on the promotion ladder for he was a Bachelor of Economics.

"The boss wants you to ring him."

"What the hell does he want now?" the Inspector asked, already frustrated. He hated being interrupted when he had already planned his morning. He took the receiver from Reynolds and dialled.

"Inspector McGuire, Sir."

"Ah, Alex. Come up to my office would you."

McGuire lifted his eyes to the heavens and breathed in deeply through his teeth, holding the receiver well away. Having regained his composure, he said, "I'll be up now, Sir."

"Hasn't he got anything better to do?" he asked Reynolds, replacing the receiver with impatience. "Doesn't he know we're busy? I've got to traipse up to his office now and I bet he could have told me what he wanted over the phone."

Reynolds smiled inwardly but made no comment. This was the Inspector's usual demeanour. He didn't suffer fools lightly – not that the Chief Super was a fool but he did sometimes get his priorities wrong and the fraud squad were overstretched this week. Their time was precious and McGuire wasn't one for idle chat.

"Enter," Chief Superintendent Spring said in reply to McGuire's knock. The DI entered the comfortable office with its *en suite* loo and wash basin, and closed the door behind him.

"Ah! Alex, sit down," the Chief said, inviting him with an open hand. McGuire sat, still not saying anything.

Swinging slightly to one side in his swivel chair the Boss, as he was affectionately known, leaned back and, with an arm of his spectacles hooked in his mouth began, "Corran. What's he up to these days?

Do we know?" The Detective Inspector bit his tongue. He'd already sent a full report on Corran for forwarding to Interpol the previous week and he could see it lying in the Chief's in-tray there in front of him. He obviously hadn't yet read it. "Wasn't Interpol interested in him at one time?"

"Yes Sir," McGuire answered, now having decided not to draw the Chief's attention to the report, knowing quite well that another twenty minutes would be taken up reading it if he did. "He's a bit iffy at the moment, Sir. We're waiting to see how things develop. Mr Corran is one of those shady characters who are just outside the reach of the long arm of the law, but we're just waiting for him to take one more step in the wrong direction. Then we'll grab him."

The senior officer didn't reveal that he had attended Corran's buffet the previous night other than to comment, "I saw PC Cord being very familiar with his daughter last night. I hope he's not getting involved. This is just an observation Alex – I don't want him blowing your investigation."

"I see," said McGuire, trying to be a little more tolerant now that he knew that the point of the conversation had been reached. "In fact, I did know about Cord – a DS saw him coming out of her flat the other night."

"What was the DS doing there?" the Chief asked, somewhat concerned at all the activity around this young lady's home.

"Eating his take-away in the car, he tells me," was the answer.

"Better keep an eye on the DS too then. Who was it by the way?"

"1226 Greg, crime squad, Sir."

The Chief took up a pen and made a note of the name. "That will be all, Alex."

"Right, Sir," McGuire said, rising to his feet.

As he opened the door to leave he turned and said, "I've sent a file to Interpol outlining Corran's activities. It's in your tray, Sir. You'll find it interesting reading."

Not waiting for the reaction, he closed the door behind him and walked back to his own office.

"I don't know," he muttered to himself. "It makes me wonder how this place runs sometimes. There's me working my balls off to get a report off to Interpol on time and he sits on it for a week while contemplating an honest, healthy lad who's just sowing his oats."

But the message hadn't fallen on deaf ears. McGuire made a mental note of the Chief's comments.

CHAPTER EIGHT

The remainder of the week was rather non-productive for Thomas, both on and off duty. He'd been able to continue with the sculpture until the Sunday afternoon. Thomas had gone to the yard and, arriving unannounced, he'd gone directly to the horses, having understood from Eric that he was free to do so at any time. The yard was quiet and unattended except for Serge Ravir. As Thomas approached the stable he startled the Frenchman who gave him the impression of being a guilty man caught on the job. But nothing seemed out of place.

"Bonjour," Thomas had greeted him politely, using his schoolboy French, but he'd been rudely ignored. He'd tried English but that got no response either. The situation was hopeless and with the man either not understanding or plainly refusing to remove the horse's blanket so that Thomas could have had a look at his subject, he gave up. He had made a quick search for Summer or Eric, but neither had been about, so he left, annoyed, frustrated and disappointed. Eric telephoned him in the evening and sounded awkward, not quite knowing how to begin. Surprisingly he didn't make any reference to the afternoon visit until Thomas mentioned it. It was then that Eric got to the point and explained that it had been Mr Corran's wish that the horse was not to be disturbed any more during the run-up to the Arc. Eric had been very apologetic, hoping the sculpture wouldn't suffer as a result. Thomas understood but couldn't help feeling put out. He telephoned Summer and told her what had been said.

"The horse is going to be whipped off to stud straight after the Arc and I can't ask Mr Corran to change his mind as he's not to know the sculpture is for him."

"To be honest," Summer said, "I don't think it was solely Mr Corran's objection. I heard Ravir telling Eric in no uncertain terms that it wasn't a good idea to have you snooping around and Eric said he'd see to it; by the way, this was all in English and Ravir speaks it very well, although he clammed up when he saw me."

Thomas's frustration turned to anger, then the policeman's mind stood back and calculated. Thinking aloud he said, "So, our foreign visitor isn't all that he'd have us believe. I see."

"Listen," Summer said, interrupting, "I've got an idea. How much more have you got to do to the sculpture?"

Thomas looked at it on the table in front of him.

"Thanks to your photos, I suppose it's virtually complete, up to the stage of casting. But when it's cast I'll have to clean up and finish off the bronze and finally check it against the horse itself. That's a critical stage – the tiniest piece of metal-run or air hole in the eyes for instance can alter the whole expression of the horse."

"In that case, why don't you come to Paris and finish it there?" she suggested with enthusiasm.

"Will you be going then?" Thomas was interested.

"I should hope so," she said. "After all, if it hadn't been for all the nursing and encouragement I gave the poor horse last year he wouldn't have raced, let alone won. He so hates flying. I do hope he doesn't get colic again this year. There's always a fear that when a horse gets it he could die."

"Can't you give them something to stop it then?" he asked, only now fully aware of the seriousness of Eyecatcher's weakness.

Summer answered him, "Well, yes, but you've got to be careful. You can't race with any trace of some substances in the blood. The horse would end up being disqualified. For instance, there's what's known as smooth muscle intestinal relaxants. They prevent bowel movement and are usually combined with a pain killer, but that's generally administered when a horse has already started the colic condition. Even then, if he gets a severe bout it takes so much out of him, he'll never be right in time to race. Last year was a miracle, and, miracles don't often repeat themselves."

"So he nearly got withdrawn," said Thomas quietly. "Well, in that case I don't see how Eric can afford not to have you on the trip."

"I hope you're right," she said, "but it's not Eric who's pulling the strings these days. By the way, did you find anything out about Mr Corran – or can't you say?"

"There is something concerning some new make-up he's unable to launch. It's left a lot of angry people in France, who are involved with the product, screaming for their money."

"Do you think there could be a genuine threat against the horse from that quarter then?" she suggested.

"Hell! Of course," said Thomas suddenly. "That's a point. The Arc would be the ideal opportunity if those Frenchmen were behind it. If only Eric would confide in me."

"Perhaps they've gone to someone higher," Summer offered. "You know, Mr Corran may have insisted, considering what's involved, and perhaps Eric doesn't want to hurt your feelings."

"Could be," he said. "I'll check it out but I would have thought it would have filtered down the channels had any threats been reported. No, I'd say it was more likely that if the threat had come from France then Corran definitely wouldn't want the police involved in case we dug too deeply for the reasons behind it. Right," he said. "About Paris. I've got some overtime due to me. I'll see if I can get it added to my leave and take it off for the Arc. I'll sort something out – promise."

"Oh, it would be marvellous," Summer replied with enthusiasm.

"I'm going to bed now. I've got an early turn in the morning," said Thomas, more down to earth. "I'll phone you tomorrow when I've got the tickets – and thanks for sorting my problems out again."

"You're welcome, love. 'Bye," she replied and put down the telephone with excitement.

The romantic idea of Paris with Thomas was appealing even though her time with him would be limited. The atmosphere there and being together would hopefully give her the opportunity to persuade him to divorce his wife and marry her. She loved him and wanted her life with him to be complete – that was her priority.

Although the romantic idea of Paris appealed to Thomas, his priority was to get the sculpture finished.

CHAPTER NINE

The next day Thomas's tour of duty was from six until two. There is no shift allowance in the force and he hated this turn. No matter how early he went to bed the previous night he'd still be tired, often over-sleeping. On the few occasions when his wife had been there, there had been no problem with the early shift. Cathy would get up before him and prepare his breakfast, something he'd never do for himself. Now he was having to leave his cup of black coffee because it was too hot and he was late. Rushing to work did nothing for public relations either. In an effort to get to the station on time, he'd be breaking speed limits which, only minutes later, he'd be trying to enforce! Too often he would arrive on the wrong side of six. This particular time Thomas made it with five minutes to spare. After being given his duties for the first half of the morning, he asked the duty sergeant if he could come back to the station at eight. There was no problem, the sergeant gave him the OK; Thomas wanted to catch the fraud squad and thought he'd mention it in case the sergeant would want to know why he was off his beat. There were only two working in the fraud department at this time, two being away, one on leave, and the other on a course.

Thomas knew how difficult it was to pin one of these detectives down. They were always out spending considerable lengths of time on investigations, travelling regularly outside the force area or with the Director of Public Prosecutions, their paperwork mounting like no others in the police force. A fraud case could take months of investigation before even an interview, let alone an arrest, was made.

Thomas was hoping that by being around from eight onwards he'd be able to catch at least one of the squad when he arrived at the office. Although they weren't due until nine, they'd often pop in just before, pick up any mail or messages and be gone before he'd have a chance to see them. When he finally did walk up the stairs to the first floor office he found he was in luck. The door was open.

"Good morning."

"Morning, Doorstop," replied Detective Sergeant Roberts, in pin-striped suit, dressed more like a business-man than a policeman. "What can I do for you today? Come into the inner sanctum."

"Ah, good," said Thomas as he entered the small room, the nickname not bothering him. He decided not to sit down, afraid he'd knock over one of the carefully prepared files which were methodically stacked on the tables and floor.

"I've been trying to catch one of you for over a week," he said. "Thatchit Corran, you know, Eye-catcher Cosmetics. Is there anything known on him or, more to the point, is he the subject of an investigation?"

"Why do you ask?" the sergeant asked cautiously.

"He's screwing the old man's daughter," said a voice from behind Thomas. It was the Detective Inspector, indicating to the DS not to say too much. Thomas turned.

"I was, or rather I did once Sir, but that's not my reason for asking. I've been told that there's been a threat against his racehorse."

"What? Kidnap, you mean?" asked the sergeant.

"No, a death threat," said Thomas, "and I was wondering if you'd heard anything about it."

"No, nothing like that. Have you asked the CID?"

"Not yet," replied Thomas.

"Well, we've heard nothing here," said Roberts, "but it wouldn't surprise me. Corran's annoyed a lot of Frenchmen and you know how hot-headed they can be. I only hope for their sake that he markets this new product of his, because if we're forced to give him a pull the whole company is going to cave in and they'll never get their money. Did you say you'd tried CID?"

"No," said Thomas, "not yet."

"Well, that's all that I can suggest. Interpol sent us an enquiry about him as you probably know, which shows he's walking a tightrope at the moment but, whichever way he falls, I can't see him being hurt. He's far too clever. However, as far as his horse is concerned, nothing's been mentioned here."

"Right," said Thomas, walking out. "Thanks, I'll try CID."

"You're welcome. Give her one for me."

Although they were all policemen, there was always interdepartmental secrecy. Thomas felt he'd been told what he needed to know and that was all, but he could see their point. There were no bigger gossips than some policemen, and a good many investigations had been blown by indiscretion.

Internal rivalry in the stations, especially the bigger ones, was nearly always apparent too. Not so much between the departments – they served the uniformed officer well whenever one called for their advice or assistance – but the rivalry existed between the uniformed squads. Thomas himself took part in it. At best it produced a healthy camaraderie, but at its worse it turned to bitchy accusations of incompetence from one squad to another.

Still on the same floor, he walked along the corridor to the CID office. On that level the floors were as bare as those downstairs, except for the rooms used by the civilian typists and clerical workers or senior officers but Thomas didn't think this particularly wrong. These people were stuck indoors for most of the day and he wouldn't want to swap his pavements for their carpets.

He'd joined the force for the variety, excitement and security the job offered (a very rare combination). He stayed because he was enjoying the complimentary front seat in the theatre of life that came with the job.

There were three doors off the corridor to the CID office. The furthest allowed access past the two secretaries, the next had direct access whilst the third, also having direct access, was superfluous and existed as a result of two rooms being knocked into one. He found this door open and entered the long room with its double row of desks, six in all, each with its own telephone which shared a common number. Windows overlooking the front of the station allowed plenty of light. There they were, eight of them, all detectives, sitting around drinking coffee. Their day didn't start until they'd had coffee. He went up to Tim Gardener with whom he got on well.

"Tim."

"Hi, Tom, what brings you up here?"

"Have there been any complaints about death threats made against a racehorse at Eric Best's stables?"

"No, why? Do you want to make one?"

Thomas smiled, "It was just something I heard."

"Has a complaint been made to you then?" Tim asked. "If you want any help just ask. I won't pinch your case from you."

"I know you wouldn't, not like some," said Thomas. "Thanks all the same but it's just something I'd been told second-hand as it were. If anything develops, I'll let you in on it, OK?"

"Yeh, anytime. Sorry I can't help."

Thomas went back downstairs, none the wiser.

He was sorely tempted to pick up the phone and ask Pamela if she knew anything but was afraid in case Ravir was there. Instead he decided to walk around to see her after his break – he'd be on town beat then. Ideal!

By eleven he had got shot of the new policewoman he'd been lumbered with to show around the town, leaving her to take a lost child back to the station. Something simple he was sure she'd be able to cope with alone.

"Excuse me, officer," a woman of about fifty called to him as she approached. "Is it all right if I park my car there? I know it says no waiting, but I'll only be five minutes."

"Yes, certainly madam," Thomas replied magnanimously.

"What if the traffic warden sees it?" she asked, sounding a little doubtful.

"It'll be all right," he reassured her, "It's the happy hour – they're at their tea break."

Preoccupied, he walked around the corner towards the hairdressers but stopped. The white Porsche was parked opposite, a warning that the Frenchman was inside. He considered tabbing the car for being parked on yellow lines but thought better of it. But he did do a police computer check on the index number over his radio. "I wonder who this is down to," he thought.

Within eight seconds he had the reply – a car hire firm in the West End of London – Hollywood Car Hire Ltd.

"It figures," he thought to himself, walking back round the corner. "Bloody poser."

CHAPTER TEN

Thomas spent that afternoon going around the travel agencies trying to book a flight to Paris which would get him there a few days before the race and return him the day after, but he didn't have a clue where he wanted to stay in Paris. He knew it would have to be somewhere near Longchamps but that was all. He'd never been to Paris before. In fact he'd never been to France before. In fear of doing the wrong thing, he decided he'd ask Summer to do the booking for him.

He walked to her house arriving just after five.

"Thomas!" she said with surprise. "What are you doing here?"

"I'm knackered," he said. "Have you got a cup of tea. I've walked round in circles all afternoon trying to book this Paris thing. Will you do it for me?"

"I don't know," she laughed. "When are you free to travel?"

"That doesn't matter really," he said. "You just book the same days as you'll be travelling and I'll arrange my time-off to suit. Where's the boy?"

"He's on a football trip with his team. Won't be back until tomorrow night – and I've got a day off tomorrow."

"Does that mean I can sleep here tonight?" Thomas asked coaxingly.

"I'm sorry love. I promised to go to a hen party tonight – pub crawling with the girls."

"How about after then?" he said.

"I thought you said you were knackered?" said Summer, pouring his tea.

"I am but I can have a kip until you come home."

"I don't fancy coming back here after a night on the booze," she said. "I'm feeling wicked, take me to your house."

"I can't do that," he said, "Cathy might turn up. You know what she's like. I know! We'll go to Richard's. He's not back until Friday. He's left me the key to check things for him."

"OK," she said, "I'll be on Coaster's Corner at midnight. Let's pretend I'm a high-class tart and you're a John picking me up."

Thomas couldn't wait. "Now how am I going to get a kip?" he said, knowing the images her idea were creating would keep him awake.

As soon as he finished his tea, Summer made him go. She didn't want him to see what she was going to wear. If he had he wouldn't have let her go out with the girls. She was going to look the part!

Thomas went home but, as he thought, he couldn't sleep. Summer's suggestion had really turned him on. He took a cold shower to try and freshen up, then tried to do some work on the sculpture but couldn't concentrate. Neither could he concentrate on the television, checking four times to make sure he had Richard's flat-key in his pocket.

The last two hours dragged. At 11.30 he was in position. The corner was quite busy with people coming out of the pubs but there was no sign of Summer. Thomas waited for about ten minutes then, deciding that he might be looking like a kerbcrawler, he moved off. He drove around past a few of the pubs and clubs hoping to see her but she wasn't about. Although it was still before the agreed time and only just approaching midnight, he drove back to the corner with the feeling that he'd been stood up. There! On the kerbside stood Summer, wearing the shortest mini he'd ever seen her in, her long, bare, shapely legs accentuated by high stiletto heels. The top of her tight red dress was backless and cut away at the sides of her breasts and she was obviously not wearing a bra. 'She never went on a pub crawl looking like that,' he thought, but he wasn't going to ask her. He didn't want to spoil the excitement. He pulled up alongside her and opened the passenger door for her to get in. When he saw her face he hesitated, thinking he was picking up the wrong girl. She was so heavily made-up, with lots of mascara and bright red lipstick. Even her hair somehow looked different, shorter – a complete transformation. He'd never seen her looking so sexy.

"What do you want me for?" she asked.

"Come on Summer, jump in," he said nervously.

"That will be £20 up front." She ran her tongue slowly and invitingly over her top lip, "Twenty pounds or I get into the car behind."

Thomas glanced in the mirror and saw there was a car parked behind, obviously looking for a pick-up.

"Christ, I don't know if I've got twenty pounds on me," he said, panicking and rummaging through his pockets. He found one £10 note and offered it to her with pleading eyes, but the only response it got was a questioning look. His gaze slid down level with her thighs – the luscious sight nearly dragged him out of the car. He looked back at her face hoping she'd release him from this torment, but she was already eyeing the car behind with a pout definitely aimed at the driver. The headlights flashed and, changing her expression to one of satisfaction, she looked down at Thomas.

"Well?"

He frantically tried his pockets again, so hot now his shirt was clinging under his armpits. Thankfully he found another £10 note and handed her the twenty. She smiled smugly, stuffed it into her clutch bag and got in. That was the first time he had driven through the town looking at a pair of legs. Summer kept up the pressure, nibbling his ear.

'God, if I'm stopped now,' he thought, hearing a police car in the distance, but he managed to arrive outside Richard's flat without meeting them. In the darkness the loud clatter of her heels broke the silence as he let her into the flat. Inside with the light on, she stood challengingly in front of him, her legs apart and ran her tongue suggestively over her top lip, again stretching his desire. He couldn't resist this anymore and held her with his hands around her buttocks pulling her in to him. She offered no resistance. Already on the brink, he discovered she wasn't wearing anything at all under the dress. The rest didn't take long . . .

When they awoke in the morning, they lay in bed realizing that Summer didn't have any other clothes to wear to go home.

"I'll fetch you some from the house," said Thomas putting his hand out for her key as she stood up.

"No, it'll be alright," she said putting all her clothes on in one movement. The sight so turned him on again that he pulled her back to the bed for an encore before tidying the flat.

"I'll wash this sheet and pillow case at home – there's mascara on them."

"Yes, I suppose they'll have to be cleaned," Thomas agreed. "I don't want Richard to know I used his bed."

He was very nervous on the journey back to Summer's house. In broad daylight she looked even more conspicuous. She eased down in the seat in an effort to hide but that merely showed more of her naked legs. Everyone Thomas hadn't seen for weeks passed him on that short journey and every traffic light was red but in the safety of Summer's house they burst into laughter. Thomas put the kettle on and prepared breakfast whilst she ran upstairs to change. Back down in jeans, she shared breakfast with him.

"How come you're off today then?" Thomas asked.

"Eric wants me to work next Sunday instead. I've got to take a gelding up North. It's broken down and the owners are having it back for the winter."

"Will it recover?"

"I should think so – it's not all that bad now. You should have been at the stables yesterday," Summer said, changing the subject. "There was one hell of a row between Corran and Eric. I thought they were going to come to blows at one time but when they realized that half the yard was listening they cooled off and went inside."

"What was it about then?" asked Thomas, interested.

"Eyecatcher, I guess," she replied, "I didn't catch the start of it but I did hear Corran saying he had to run at all costs, that there was more than the prize money at stake as he well knew and that if the horse didn't win he'd take Eric down with him."

"Eric seemed both threatened and angry. He said that if the horse wasn't one hundred per cent, then no way was he going to run him. It wasn't worth killing the horse for some bet he probably wasn't going to land anyway. 'Some bet! Some bet!' Corran was shouting. 'Do you realize how much money I've had to spread to keep Interpol off my back. If I don't land this touch you'll lose this stable. Don't forget you begged me for a piece of the action in 'Smudge'. If the French producers find out what's up before I can find a buyer we'll have to leave the country and run. I'm not doing time for a fucking horse. The money from the French is all staked on this one race. If the result is right the stake goes back to the producers with an apology – end of story. If not, you get the blame. Remember your name is on the British directorship. I'm just on the French side.' That's all I heard before they went inside," Summer said, "but I thought Corran was going to explode. His face was like thunder."

"Hell, I didn't know that," Thomas said thinking how close to the chest the fraud squad had held their cards.

"Where was Ravir when this was going on?"

"No idea," said Summer, "but he wasn't around."

Thomas remembered – he knew where Ravir had been.

"This isn't doing the stable morale any good," she said. "The lads were talking all afternoon about it. I'm glad I'm not there today. What shift are you supposed to be?"

"Nights," he said wearily.

"Come on then. Help me to wash the dishes and then you can curl up on the settee for a couple of hours. I've got some shopping to do. I'll wake you at one – how's that?" Summer offered kindly.

"Thanks," he said and smiled like a spoilt cat.

CHAPTER ELEVEN

When Thomas arrived at the station that night, there was a message taped on his locker. "Phone Eric."

He went to the charge room and telephoned the stables.

"Hi," Eric said, giving no sign of the previous day's showdown. "Do you fancy going racing tomorrow?"

Thomas was silent for a second or two, taken aback by the seeming change of heart the invitation signalled.

"Um . . . Um . . . Sure, great," he said. "Where? When?"

"Be at the yard by nine. We'll go up in my car. We've got two horses going at Newmarket. One should win. Oh, and don't be late."

"Right," said Thomas, still a bit lost for words "I'll look forward to it. See you at nine then."

During that night Thomas considered the change of attitude. Had Eric realized that he had upset him by preventing him from seeing Eyecatcher at the stable yard, or was it that he wanted an opportunity to tell him about the threats? Or was he fishing to find out how much he knew about the row with

Corran, presuming Summer had overheard and told him? It was sure to be one of these reasons, he thought, but he intended to play along. After all, he enjoyed the few opportunities he had to go racing with a trainer. He liked the feeling it gave him of being on the inside, occasionally being introduced to the jockeys and other trainers and hopefully picking up information about their horse's chances. But most of all he liked to have a bet on a horse that he knew from the trainer's mouth was for all intents and purposes going to win. This gave him a big buzz.

Struggling to stay awake, cold, and his eyes itching from tiredness, Thomas was at the yard at nine prompt. Everyone was busy, either mucking out, carrying hay or filling water buckets.

"Morning, Sir," one or two greeted. Thomas, saying 'morning' back, was never sure if the acknowledgement was meant for him or for the owner they thought he might be.

Eric walked across the yard towards him, racing silks over his arm.

"Right, let's go. If we've got time, we'll stop for a spot of breakfast on the way. The horses have already left. I like them to get to the course at least three hours before the race. That way I can settle them down and get the declarations in on time."

Thomas settled down with a copy of *The Sporting Life* in the passenger seat of Eric's BMW. He already knew that one of the runners was Sparrow Hawk, carrying a penalty for its last win. The other was a two-year-old filly called Tearful, who was going in the first, the two o'clock and had obvious claims on her form. She'd won her last two races and had been second in the previous one. She was also carrying the champion jockey. Reading the proposed starting prices, Thomas could see that she was even-money favourite.

"Sparrow Hawk's the one," Eric said, reading Thomas's mind. "Forget the filly – she won't like the ground. Won't be in the first three. She likes it really hard."

"Don't they all," joked Thomas.

He switched his attention to Sparrow Hawk's race, the three o'clock. The forecast price was 8/1 and only one correspondent had tipped him.

"Are you sure he'll win, Eric?"

"He'll walk it. Don't bother with an each way bet, have him to win."

"Should I take a price?" asked Thomas.

"If you can get 8/1 or better. It's up to you but I think that's about his value. You'll have to excuse me when we get there. Tearful's owners will be expecting me to spend time with them."

"What about Sparrow Hawk's owners?" Thomas asked.

"That's no problem. I own him. I originally bought him for an accountant in Hong Kong but he jibbed out leaving me with the auctioneer's bill of £22,000. Fancy buying it?"

"Me? You're kidding. I couldn't afford that kind of money."

"Get a few policemen together and form a syndicate. It won't be so bad then."

Thomas thought the chances unlikely and left it at that.

"I hope my phone call didn't upset you the other day," Eric turned to Thomas.

"Well, I was disappointed more than anything. I

didn't think my presence was unsettling the horse. You've never mentioned it before," Thomas replied.

"It's not my decision. You know if it were up to me – well, what I'm trying to say is, don't take it personally. It's just Mr Corran being over-protective but, as he pays the bills, I have to abide by his wishes. It won't spoil the sculpture will it, I mean it's ready for casting now, isn't it?"

"Yes, but there's still a lot of work to be done. What are the chances of seeing him again, if I need to, after casting? Corran doesn't have to know," Thomas suggested.

"Very slim," said Eric seriously. "Ravir is bound to tell Corran and he'd go berserk like he did yesterday. Did Summer tell you?"

Thomas was nearly caught out, his wits dulled by tiredness, "Yeh, um, no. She said something about you two arguing, but said it was the pressures of the big race looming up. I think she was trying to find an excuse, thinking that you had upset me. No, don't worry about it, honestly," Thomas went on, "there's bound to be conflict between an owner and trainer. I should imagine it's like a mother and a foster-mother arguing over which is the best way to bring up baby."

Eric had not heard it put quite like that before and wasn't sure if it was a good simile or not.

"No hard feelings then, Thomas," he said, brushing it aside.

Thomas wanted to ask about Ravir but was too tired to think straight. He tried to concentrate on the runners in the first race but his eyes kept mixing up the lines. He closed them briefly and fell asleep. Eric gave him a sideways glance and relaxed with a faint smile. He was satisfied that Thomas's suspicions hadn't been aroused.

It was the BMW easing to a silent standstill that woke Thomas. He had slept soundly right through the journey and now at Newmarket, with half-closed eyes, he peered through the rain running down the windscreen, gently easing himself upright as he tried to get his bearings.

"What time is it?" Thomas yawned.

"Eleven fifteen. Had a good sleep?" Eric asked.

"Yeah. Waw, I needed that!" he said, now fully awake. He looked around, unfamiliar with the surroundings. "What happened to breakfast?"

"Oh, it seemed a pity to wake you. Never mind, you'll be able to find something here. Fit then?" Eric said jauntily opening the door and taking documents out of the glove compartment. He handed Thomas an umbrella from the boot and took one for himself. Together they walked quickly across the car park.

Eric, being much shorter, reminded Thomas of a jockey, but Thomas knew he had no such background. He had been a farmer's son, had done well at school and had gone on to veterinary college. But the premature death of his father at forty-three had caused him to curtail his studies before his final year, and return to the farm which expanded and grew prosperous under Eric's management – until the government's milk quota policy forced him to change direction. He had been a successful permit-holder racing two hunter chasers and it had seemed a natural step to progress into National Hunt training. He took out a full trainer's licence, selling the farm and buying a small yard. He immediately experienced phenomenal success which took him, in only his second season, to the top of the trainer's table. Looking for bigger pickings, Eric moved at great expense to larger and more fashionable premises and turned completely to flat racing. He didn't find adapting to the change easy, struggling to keep his head above water as he desperately tried to hang on to his owners and find new ones who'd be willing to take a chance on his ability to train flat-racing horses. But his second season had brought him Eyecatcher. The rest would be history one day.

The travelling lad was waiting for them. He had a weatherbeaten complexion – and yet a cheeky boyish face – something like an old, cooking-apple. At a guess Thomas put him at around fifty, but he may have been a lot younger.

Thomas had gathered a general knowledge of training methods but he knew very little about the finer points of the vocation. One things he just couldn't fathom out nor could ever find a satisfactory explanation to was why horses were awakened to be trained so early in the morning – usually before dawn (in the case of the National Hunt, an icy cold dawn) – and allowed to rest in the afternoon, which must have been as foreign to them as night shift was to Thomas. Then, having ajusted to this routine, the odd day came when they were suddenly prevented from resting as they'd learnt to expect in the afternoon and, instead, be asked to partake in the most energy-sapping experience they were ever likely to encounter – a race! Thomas thought it logical that if a horse were to be at his best for a race in the afternoon then it would benefit from being trained in the afternoon, an exercise which would also benefit some of their human caretakers if the craggy, weather-beaten looks were anything to go by.

"How did they travel?" Eric enquired.

"Well Sir, very well. That Sparrow Hawk's a proper Christian. Let you do anything to him. Just had the blacksmith re-shoe his off fore, and, do you know, old Sparrow even put his foot out for him."

They all three laughed but Thomas was at a bit of a disadvantage, not knowing the horse.

"OK," said Eric eager to get on with things. "Here are the passports," handing them to the lad. "Get them in and nicely settled. I'll go and declare." Turning to Thomas he said, "I'll have to leave you for the time being, but if I don't see you before, we'll meet at three in the trainer's stand. Here," he said and tied a day badge to Thomas's button-hole.

"Thanks," said Thomas, fully appreciating the entrance fee the badge was going to save him. "See you at three then," he said and walked away towards the members' entrance with no idea of what he was going to do for the next three hours or so before the first race. Once on the course, he walked about aimlessly. Even the bookies hadn't put up their pitches yet. The catering was nowhere near being ready although it did look as if he could have had a drink if he wanted. Instead he decided to have a browse through the course museum.

When he came out the rain was still falling quite heavily. He eventually found himself in the bar, bought a bottle of beer, which was served to him with its cap replaced by an inverted plastic glass, and sat down. Heavily pushing back on the chair and stretching out his legs, he felt hungry but was now comfortable and too tired to bother to get any food.

Daydreaming, Thomas hardly noticed the bar filling up or the rain stopping. When he had finished his drink he looked at the time. It was 1.15. Taking advantage of the break in the weather, he went down to one of the small book-stands outside and purchased a race-form card which endorsed Eric's warning about Tearful. Thomas read, ". . . acts well on firm going – yet to run on soft – should improve."

Turning to the three o'clock he found the comments on Sparrow Hawk more exciting, ". . . bay colt, formally trained by V. Arnold – has shown much improved form as a 4-year-old, winning his last race on good going by 8 lengths – will stay 1½ miles." But when Thomas worked through the ratings he found Sparrow Hawk to be down 6 points behind the favourite who had won its last two races. There were also two other last-time-out winners in the field. Counting his money without removing his hand from his pocket he walked to the betting office for the opening show, but there was none on offer, so with the time now at 1.50, he walked to the Silver Ring. The bookies had Tearful opening at 7/2. It stayed there for some time but next showed shorter at 3/1. He saw one or two punters putting on a couple of hundred pounds each. The price remained at 3/1. 'Suckers,' he thought, with the advantage of his inside knowledge, but even then he had no idea of what to back instead. He felt it necessary to have a bet on something but before he could make a decision they were off and running.

Tearful broke well and stayed in front until the last hundred yards where it was just overtaken to lose in the photofinish. Thomas didn't feel so cocky now. What am I to interpret from that, he thought. He knew that Eric wouldn't have deliberately misled him – there would be no point, but surely the going wasn't false and if Tearful had been suited by it then what of Sparrow Hawk? However, there was another way of looking at it which suggested that the stable was so much in form that Sparrow Hawk was going to be one hell of a bet. He counted his money again and worked out that he'd have to lay about £20 win and £5 each way to win enough for his Paris trip. The each way was an insurance in case the horse only finished placed (after all, Tearful hadn't run to plan).

No sooner had the 'Weigh In' been announced than the runners for the next race were on the way to the start. This time Thomas made his mind up quickly, risking £2 on the favourite at even money and £2 each way on a 5/1 chance. Stupid bet, he thought after placing it. The favourite finished third and the 5/1 shot was in the pack. He was angry with himself for not waiting – the £6 he had just lost could have gone on Sparrow Hawk.

It was 2.50, the rain returned and he started looking for Eric. On his way, he made a small diversion to the paddock area, wanting a close-up look at Sparrow Hawk before placing his bet. He hadn't seen the horse before, it being a fairly new addition to the yard. When Thomas did see it being led around by the lad, he looked in open-mouthed disbelief – it was the spitting image of Eyecatcher! He waited for the big bay to go round again. It had no white about it, nothing to distinguish him from his double, except that he did hold his head low, but then the rain was lashing down. Was this Eyecatcher, he thought? Was this the reason for the recent events? Was this why he had been invited – to be innocently roped-in on a coup? Surely they wouldn't dare, not with such a famous horse but then again, who'd dare believe they'd try. He walked across to the bookies in the ring. The betting had opened. Thomas looked around quickly but there was no sign of Eric. Rushing now, he was uncertain whether to have a bet or not. An announcement was made over the public address system – the going had been changed to heavy and an inspection was going to be made after the next race to consider abandoning the meeting. The rain could now certainly be described as torrential. The bookies doggedly stuck to their pitches as their chalked-up prices were being washed away, and it appeared as if the start was being delayed. No explanation was given for the late off and with the horses now already at the post Thomas could only assume that it was because of the adverse weather conditions. A sudden decrease in the force of the rain encouraged the bookmakers to make another attempt at opening the market.

"Six to one the field," they shouted. "Six to one the field."

Thomas looked at a number of the boards. Sparrow Hawk had opened at 6/1 co-favourite with two others, but was now 8/1. The other two had shortened to 5/1 joint favourites. Thomas approached bookie after bookie to try to get his each-way bet on, but no-one was taking each ways. There was now a clear favourite at 9/2, the other dropping half a point to 11/2. Sparrow Hawk had drifted out to 10/1.

'Hell, where's Eric,' he thought, 'nobody seems to want Sparrow Hawk.'

"They're under orders" came over the public

address. In panic Thomas put £25 to win at 10/1 and immediately regretted it. The market leaders shortened even further. He took his betting ticket and ran to the shelter of the stands, just in time for the off. Visibility was poor but when they came into view it appeared to be Sparrow Hawk who was in the lead by about ten to twelve lengths and increasing. At the halfway stage he was still there and Thomas feared the horse had shot his bolt but there was no sign of him getting caught. He was pounding on relentlessly. With a furlong to go, he was in front by about 20 lengths with the jockey looking over both shoulders for any dangers. As none existed the jockey seemed to ease the horse up until he was slowly lobbing, but trying to catch him was a forlorn hope as he still won with ridiculous ease. The return starting price surprised Thomas for it was only 6/1, but he was full of excitement, his apprehension quickly forgotten. £250! Great! That would pay for Paris. As he walked down the steps to get his money, the dreaded announcement over the public address brought him quickly back down to earth.

"Stewards' enquiry."

"Balls!" he muttered to himself, and thought again of the uncanny similarity between Sparrow Hawk and Eyecatcher – a resemblance which he feared hadn't passed unnoticed by the stewards either. Eric wouldn't pull such an amateurish stunt, he thought to himself. Then the fog of panic began to clear as he weighed up the facts. Suddenly the solution shone through. Eycatcher would never have won in that manner, no matter how poor the opposition. A short head cat-and-mouse would have been his finish, not an ever extending 20 lengths. He didn't have to wait long to have his answer ticked, the public address announcement declared, "The stewards's enquiry concerns the second and fourth horse . . . There's an objection. The fourth horse objects to the second."

At that moment Eric materialized, calling to Thomas from the top of the stand. Thomas climbed up and together they went down the other side to the winner's enclosure.

"Well, did you have a good bet?"

"Yes," answered Thomas, unable to hide his pleasure. "I had £25 on at 10/1."

"10/1, you jammy sod, how did you manage to get that price?" asked Eric.

"I waited until they were under orders," Thomas replied. "I would have put more on but with all that mud I wasn't sure, and I couldn't find you for your advice. Where the hell were you?"

"I'm sorry," Eric apologized, "only I was waylaid by the bloody TV fellow – what's his name – for an up-date on Eyecatcher's chances for next week's big 'un."

"How did Sparrow Hawk shorten so rapidly to 6/1 on the off?" asked Thomas.

"Oh, that was probably my fault," confessed Eric. "I tipped it on the box. He must have loved the ground, but now the handicapper will probably punish him."

After the stewards' enquiry into the objection the result remained unaltered. Thomas went to collect his winnings, leaving Eric to go on to receive his trophy and congratulations. The press circled him and Thomas distinctly heard one of them ask.

"Mr Best, is it true that there have been threats to kill Eyecatcher?"

Thomas turned but couldn't see Eric's face for a reaction and he wasn't close enough to hear the reply. He'd have to wait and scan the papers the following morning.

A little damp but £250 richer, Thomas was bright and cheerful on the return journey.

"I wanted to get away quickly," said Eric, a little out of breath, "to avoid the mass exodus if the stewards abandon the meeting."

"Thanks for the day out, Eric. I enjoyed it despite the rain."

"Good, I'm glad," Eric smiled at him. "Pity I couldn't spend more time with you, but that's how it is sometimes."

As the conversation petered out, Thomas became bored with the motorway scenery, and looked about him for something to read. The horse passports were on the dashboard. Picking them up he said, "Mind if I look at these? I've never actually seen one before."

"Help yourself," Eric replied, keeping his eyes on the road in front of him.

Thomas picked up the two books. They each had twenty pages, approximately three inches by six inches, and both were covered in black plastic. From the outside they were identical and, except for the different horse's name which had been written on labels stuck to the front covers, plain. He opened Sparrow Hawk's. On the first page which, like the rest, was of cartridge-type paper, Thomas read the printed words:

"Document of Description of the Identification of

Foals and Yearlings, Race Horses, Brood Mares and Stallions."

The same was repeated in French underneath and below that the addresses of the Racing Authorities of Great Britain, Ireland and France. Turning the pages he could see that pages 2, 3, 4 and 5 were completely full of general instructions for vets, trainers, breeders and shipping agents. On pages 6 and 7 the horse's vaccinations particulars were entered. Page 8 was more like a car log book with the previous and current keepers of the horse, owners and, more recently, trainers. Eric's name was the last entry. It was page 9 that was odd and aroused Thomas's interest. It was the facing side of the centre pages of the book, which looked as if they had been stapled in after the passport itself had been assembled. This appeared particularly so, since pages 8 and 12 looked as if they were the original centre pages, both having been set aside for the owner and trainer's logs. Looking at what were now the centre pages, he could see they were a different shade of white and of slightly heavier cartridge paper. Both top and bottom edges of the pages were about a quarter inch shorter than the rest of the book and serrated like broken perforations. They were both printed and had hand written entries but it was easy to see from the hand-writing that they were not original but a double-sided photocopy bearing only the Weatherby's pressure-embossed stamp for authenticity, but it was so faint it was almost indiscernible. Comparing it with Tearful's passport Thomas was satisfied that the centre pages were similarly prepared. He asked, "Are all passports the same?"

"More or less," answered Eric. "Weatherby's re-designed the centrefold to make it neater but they didn't withdraw the former design, merely superceded it. So there are still some old passports about. Both those you've got there are the recent type."

He closed Tearful's and concentrated on Sparrow Hawk's page 9, reading the passport number and breeding details. Turning over, the centre fold was now in front of him. In order to read it the right way up, he had to turn the passport through ninety degrees. The staples were now running from left to right, halfway down the double page. The top half depicted various outline diagrams of a horse in standing position and fully showed both its left and right sides. Underneath these there were section outlines of a horse's head and muzzle, a rear view of its front legs and a complete rear view of its hind-quarters. The remaining bottom half below these diagrams was set out in the form of a certificate for the written description of the horse and the particulars to be entered. Four printed instructions on the page read:—

1 Written descriptions should be typed or written in block capitals.
2 Written description and diagram should agree.
3 All white markings should be hatched in red.
4 Whorls must be shown thus, 'X', and described below in detail.

There were printed sections where the colour, sex, year of birth, sire, dam and blood group of the horse were to be entered. He understood this to be a marking certificate. There was a further instruction which read: 'White markings to be shown in red'.

There weren't any, which meant that Sparrow Hawk was all bay and had no white markings. 'That's probably why he looked so much like Eyecatcher,' he thought. In the section 'Acquired Marks', none had been entered. Thomas took this to mean injury marks. There were four little crosses marked on the diagrams, one at the base of the neck right side, and another on the left, closer to the withers. He saw the other two were positioned one above the other on what he'd describe as the back of the right foreleg. He read that these little crosses depicted whorls. "What are whorls?" he asked.

"They're difficult to explain really without showing you," Eric answered. "I suppose you could describe them as little circular partings in a horse's hair. Their position and frequency varies to such an extent that they are considered as unique as fingerprints, and the most reliable method of indentification one can apply to a horse. The method is accepted by Weatherby's who have adopted it."

"Can't they be permed out or lacquered or something?" asked Thomas.

"No," said Eric, quite definitely. "They're permanent."

"This horse only seems to have four," remarked Thomas.

"I've known some horse's passports to read none and others to have a lot more. Sometimes a horse's colour doesn't show them up clearly, so that if the light is poor the vet can miss the odd one or two, but in general they're pretty foolproof."

"Does a vet have to fill out this description then?" Thomas asked.

"Yes, it's got to be done by a vet – less chance of

fiddling I suppose. If a vet was caught trying to fiddle them I should imagine he'd get struck off. Weatherby's have got things pretty tight, even down to the blood grouping now."

Thomas didn't consider it pretty tight. He could visualize the procedure; the vet probably filled in a description form which he would forward to Weatherby's who in turn photocopied it and inserted the photocopy into the passport. The vet's original was probably retained and filed by them. The copy seemed poor security. After all, Thomas thought, to forge one of those, all one would have to do would be to mask out what was needed to be altered and insert the false information and re-photocopy it onto a similar piece of cartridge paper. Any of the modern plain-paper photocopiers with the black carbon toner system, like the one in the police station, would do the job without a problem and be able to reproduce both sides on the one page. The paper embossing stamp would be no problem to acquire either. Thomas recalled how he had once enquired how difficult it would be to have one of these made up; it was an embossing on a garage MOT certificate he'd suspected to be false. The suppliers had discussed the matter with him and said that it would be possible for anyone to have whatever stamp they wanted made up, and if this was ordered personally and paid for in cash, then the customer would be pretty well untraceable. However, they did say that a request for a government stamp bearing a crest or coat of arms, no matter what nationality, would be looked at with suspicion unless it was accompanied by the appropriate documentation. Since his enquiry the suppliers had promised to tighten up on the MOT stamps, but Thomas reckoned that an order for this stamp in front of him would need only a little nonchalance.

'That could easily have been Eyecatcher at Newmarket,' he thought, but kept his feelings to himself. He scanned through the remainder of the passport, the pages for inspection by the racing authorities, presumably, a record of the horse made when it arrived at a race course, and finally movements abroad and customs visas. Impressive and authoritative as the passport was, Thomas considered that its weakness was definitely in the centre-spread marking certificate. What was the point of bothering to disguise a horse, or even finding a ringer when all that was necessary was to forge the descriptive form? Unless, of course, Weatherby lodged original descriptive forms with the officials at the meeting where a horse was to race. Then they could be compared for authenticity when produced for declaration on the day. He replaced the passports and leaned back. The rain had finally stopped and the teatime sky was breaking into a promise of a pleasant evening.

Their arrival at the yard showed it to be in much the same way as they had left it. It was feeding time. The staff had already heard the results and the pleasure the success had brought showed on their faces. Summer, with two empty buckets in her hands, stood with a grin as they walked over to the house.

"When you've finished that," Eric said to her, "pop in the house and see that Thomas has a cup of tea. I'll be with you in a moment." He walked on.

Thomas stopped as he reached Summer, "No thanks Summer, I've got to get back home. I'm on duty again tonight. Thanks again," he shouted to Eric as he watched him walk into his office.

Eric raised his hand in acknowledgement. "You're welcome," he said and disappeared.

"Do you want a quick sneak at Eyecatcher before you go?" Summer asked Thomas.

"Why? Is he here?" Thomas asked almost disbelievingly.

"Of course he's here," she said, "Where did you think he'd be?" she smiled quizzically.

"Oh, it's nothing, just a theory I had," he mumbled.

"Well, do you want a peep or not?"

"No, I'd better not," he finally answered.

"OK then, I won't keep you," she said giving him a peck on his nose. "Phone me tomorrow. I should have your tickets by then."

Thomas told her about his win before pecking her in return. Then he got into his car and drove away. At the crossroads a mile away, he saw the transporter bringing Tearful and Sparrow Hawk back home. Smiling to himself he thought, 'It's about time I forgot that I'm a policeman and learnt to relax on my days off.'

CHAPTER TWELVE

That night, Thomas and Richard were back on duty together. There had been a lot of thefts of radios from vehicles parked in public house car parks and their instructions for the night were to use an unmarked van and park in a suitable place in the hope of catching the thieves.

They settled in and prepared for a long night, knowing that the ear pieces they had fitted to the police radio wouldn't let them drop off to sleep. The two policemen had chosen the car park of a large pub which was running a disco until 1 am. It was packed but their choice was influenced by their liking for the music that drifted out into the open air.

"How did the holiday go?" Thomas asked.

"Brilliant," said Richard, his brown face endorsing the answer.

"What does your fiancee say about your foreign binges?"

"She's gone back to university so there was no need to tell her."

"No need to tell her? You wait till she sees your suntan."

"She'll be so pleased to see me, she won't notice,"

laughed Richard. "Did I miss anything when I was away?"

"Not really," answered Thomas. "It's been busy, but not spectacular."

"Any news on the cultures?" asked Richard, trying to prompt him into saying something of interest.

"Smudge, you mean?" Thomas paused and thought. "No, there's been no further developments with the fraud squad to my knowledge but whether the situation is hotting up in France is a different matter. Corran is aware of Interpol's interest in him, though – I know that much. There was an open argument between Eric and Corran at the yard the day before yesterday which suggests that there are disagreements over Eyecatcher amongst other things."

"How did they behave at the New Ritz?" Richard asked.

"In front of the guests they were full of praise and congratulations for one another, but offstage I noticed a definite rift. Good job the band didn't strike up the Conga, as I wouldn't have known which snake I was supposed to latch on to."

"As bad as that was it?" remarked Richard.

"Well, maybe not that bad. It's just that I'm disappointed with Eric for not confiding in me over the Eyecatcher death threats and then not letting me see the horse for the final work on the sculpture. He'd been told by Corran that the horse wasn't to be disturbed."

"How's the sculpture been going, then?" Richard asked. "You should have made enough by now to buy a decent car instead of that little toy you've got," he teased.

"Don't you make fun of my car, mate. That particular model's a true British classic, not like that foreign junk you've got and, while we're about it, I only make four hundred pounds out of those sculptures for about two months work. After I've paid for casting and travelling, I don't make a fortune."

"I only asked how the sculpture was coming," said Richard, laughing at his friend's reaction.

"Up to now, Eyecatcher's the best I've done. All I hope is that it casts well," said Thomas, looking slightly worried.

"When are you hoping to have it cast then?"

"This Saturday."

"Aye. By the way, you haven't seen my pillow case anywhere have you?" Richard looked at him.

"Shush!" Thomas whispered.

A Ford XR3 with four youths inside cruised slowly around the car park. The policemen watched in silence, both noting down the number, but after two circuits it sped away.

"What did you think?" asked Richard.

"Could be," said Thomas. "We'll check it later."

Relaxing again they started a game to pass the time. Richard began.

"You wake up in a strange bed and look at your watch. You're on a 9 to 5 shift and it's five to nine. You jump out of bed and rush into your uniform but you can only find one boot. The other just isn't there. You know that if you are not in work within half an hour the station telephones your home or calls to check on you. Your wife is there and thinks you haven't been home all night because you've worked a doubler. Do you:

(a) Go on duty with only one boot and claim someone just pinched the other as you were adjusting your socks in the locker room.
(b) Go on duty with no boots at all and say it's part of a sponsored charity walk, or
(c) Go back to sleep and hope it's only eight o'clock and the boot will be there when you wake up the next time."

Before Thomas could choose or offer an even better excuse, the radio interrupted

"Control to Zero Two – fire service in attendance at 2 Full Road."

"That's Jed Evans, the vet," said Thomas, "I hope they're all right. They're most likely to be in bed at this time of night."

Thomas listened anxiously but because control were not using an open channel, he was restricted to hearing only half of the conversation, the other being bleeped out. Fire tenders were being sent to the scene and, from the messages, it seemed as if nobody was sure if the premises was occupied or not and, if so, by how many. He informed control of the fact that Jed Evans and his mother were usually at the address and offered to attend. A long two minutes later the reply returned.

"Negative Zulu 4, you are to remain at your position. Your assistance is not required."

Thomas and Richard felt helpless as they listened in for the next five minutes. Someone at the scene of the fire had been taken to hospital. Further details had not been given over the air. They remained in the car park for another boring, uncomfortable hour until they were stood down. All they prayed for on the return journey to the police station was that no thefts would be reported from the car park they'd just left during the time they'd been there.

1am was refreshment time. Thomas and Richard found Phil Cousins in the canteen. He had attended at the fire.

"What happened?" Thomas asked him as he pulled up a chair to share his table.

"Looks like a burglary, definite arson and maybe a murder. Scene of crime are there now. They're waiting for forensic. The place is cordoned off," PC Cousins answered matter-of-factly.

"Whose murder?" Thomas asked, concerned.

"The old lady's if she doesn't pull through. Chances are slim, she's on a respirator. Took in a lot of fumes and smoke. She was unconscious when the firemen found her."

"What about the son, Jed?"

"He's OK," said Phil. "Came home soon after the fire brigade arrived. It was a neighbour who raised the alarm. Good job – saved some of the house but the two front rooms and hall were pretty bad. The seat of the fire seemed to be in a store room or dispensary. You know the people do you?"

"Yes," Thomas said, getting up to open a tin of baked beans he had brought to work with two slices of bread for toasting. There was no food available in the canteen on nights, but the facilities were left open for the shift to help themselves. He heated the beans and put the bread under the grill.

"What's the score on the burglary?" asked Richard, tucking into his sandwiches.

"Don't know much," Phil answered. "Looks like they had a go at the drugs cabinet though. The fire was probably started to destroy the evidence. What I can't understand is how the old lady didn't hear anything."

"Because she's as deaf as a post," Thomas explained. He thought he'd better call on Jed in the morning to see how his mother was.

CHAPTER THIRTEEN

Unfortunately, Thomas slept until 12.30 the following morning, but he didn't have to go out of his way to see Jed Evans – he was already at the police station when he came on duty at 2pm. He met him by the double doors at the back entrance.

"How's your mother?" Thomas asked him, aware of how the recent tragedy had seemed to have knocked the stuffing out of the usually robust vet.

At that moment, a number of PC's coming on duty walked into the station, one of them passed behind Thomas and whispered "Dummy" loud enough for only him to hear. Shit, he thought, but the dummy remained in Thomas's pocket. He'd have to pay the pound.

"A lot better thanks. She's off the danger list. I'm going to see her now actually. I've just been giving statements to your CID."

"What exactly happened?" asked Thomas.

"Well, I came home at about 11.30. I'd been to Eric Best's yard – last minute rush to get a health certificate done for Eyecatcher before France. I'd had trouble with a foaling in the morning and it had made all my day run late. Anyhow, when I got in, Mam said there had just been a telephone call. Whoever it was wanted me to attend to a dog which had been run over in Broomstown Estate. Well that's nearly eight miles away. She had told the man that I wasn't a canine veterinary anymore but he told her that the police had been to the accident and had instructed him to ask me to attend. Apparently this wasn't true – there wasn't an accident reported. I went to Broomstown but, needless to say, there was no dog and no caller." Jed took a deep shaky breath and, his composure restored, continued. "When I got back the place was on fire and the rest you probably know." Jed's eyes were distant, inwardly recalling the events.

"You're mother didn't recognise the caller I suppose?" asked Thomas.

"No," said Jed. "All she said before I went was that she thought he was foreign but she wasn't sure. Anyway you must excuse me. I've got to go and see her."

"Of course," said Thomas. "Give her my best wishes. Tell her I'll visit her as soon as she's well enough."

Thomas watched Jed walk out of the station and then he went to see if he could get an update on the burglary and arson from the incident room. Passing him in the corridor, DC Tim Gardener saved him the trouble.

"Tim! Just the man. Any developments on last night's fire at Full Road?"

"Hi, Thomas. Not much. There's a team been doing house to house enquiries but I haven't been to the incident room as yet so I don't know if there are any firm leads. But we've got a pile of actions to follow up. Let's hope there's a break-through. You know them don't you?"

"Yes," said Thomas. "What was the motive?"

"Burglary, no doubt about it, but for what, we can't be sure as yet. It could be money, anything, only the drugs cabinet was forced open. Forensic are looking at it now to establish if it burst open with the intense heat or if an instrument was used."

"Any ideas what started the fire?" Thomas queried.

"Hard to tell," said Tim. "It started in a downstairs front room – I believe it was a storeroom or something. Apparently full of papers, drugs, animal treatments, even meths."

"I know that room well," said Thomas. "One match would have been enough and there'd be no need for a forced entry. The front door is always open."

"We've interviewed the son," Tim continued. "He's off the hook. Feeling was that he may have done it to destroy accounts to dodge the taxman but, thankfully for him, his mother has regained consciousness and supports his story, although the phone call about the accident may be just a coincidence and unconnected."

"Oh! I'm sorry," he said, "I haven't told you about the phone call."

"It's OK," said Thomas. "Jed Evans spoke to me about that five minutes ago."

"So there you have it," said Tim. "You know as much as I do at the moment."

"Thanks. I hope we catch the bastard that's all."

They parted company with the same objective.

Chemist shop break-ins for controlled drugs were

a frequent occurrence. But a vet's surgery, that was something new. What drugs would a vet keep Thomas thought – pethadin, amphetamin, barbiturates, morphine? They'd use all those, and with many a surgery not alarmed and separated from living quarters, he concluded that a vet's would be easy meat for drug stealers. But this line of thought didn't help him. He couldn't bring to mind any suspects, and the hours of house-to-house calls that followed to see potential witnesses and neighbours who had been out previously when the police called, failed to gain any advances towards solving the mystery.

Mainly due to the bitter lessons learnt from the 'Yorkshire Ripper' investigations, it had been introduced, recognised and accepted countrywide that the only proper way to investigate a major crime was by a system which had been developed to be compatible with all police computers in Great Britain. This meant that, if necessary, one force could marry the information it had gleaned to that of any other force investigating a similar incident. Basically, the backbone of the method was good, old-fashioned, house-to-house enquiries, but the new approach was so thorough and professional that the police could be reasonably confident that their man was in the system somewhere, waiting for the computer to hook his name out of the sea of information. In the old days many criminals could escape the net.

Immediately following a major crime, the system was put into operation. Initially an incident room would be set up, staffed by specially trained officers who had been taken from their normal duties for the investigation. This room was set up as close to the scene of the crime as practicable, usually at the local police station. Then teams, normally consisting of two officers, would be taken off their regular duties and employed to physically listcheck and account for every place of abode in the direct vicinity of the crime. These lists then went to the incident room where they were further delegated to teams whose job it was to list and account for every occupant in each dwelling. Each occupant would then be interviewed by way of a questionnaire relevant to the crime being investigated. All this information was returned to the incident room, fed into the computer and cross referenced throughout. If anything came to the fore which a team officer, or for that matter any policeman, considered worthy of further interest, he or she would put the information, which was now termed as an 'Action', on a small report and either log or telephone it through to the incident room for the attention of the CID officers to follow up. The system would spread outwards from the location of the crime like a leaking pen in a shirt pocket and was a big drain on police resources.

Thomas hoped for a breakthrough soon. He didn't want this new threat of leave-cancellation hanging over him just before Paris.

CHAPTER FOURTEEN

Thomas made arrangements to go to the foundry to get his sculpture cast at the weekend. The men looked forward to seeing him, knowing it meant a change of routine. Casting a horse was far more interesting and more challenging to the craftsman than the run-of-the-mill bolt or machine parts. Thomas always tried to be present at the casting, supervising as best as he could, but the expertise of the foundrymen often made him feel inadequate.

Bill, the head foundryman, knew his trade well. With critical admiration, he examined the sculpture. He wasn't a sculptor, but had often offered Thomas advice to get the optimum results out of the final bronze.

"Damn, this is good Tom. That's Eyecatcher all right," Bill said, turning it over in his hands before putting it down on a table in front of him and standing back. "Bet you won't want to part with this one once it's finished. How many do you want?"

"Just the one," Thomas replied, flattered by the compliments. "I can't afford to have spares."

"Right, let's get to work," said Bill, standing up. "Have you brought the wax cast?"

The cast, which was an identical copy of the clay

original, was the result of days of work and patience. To produce a wax image of Eyecatcher, Thomas first had to make a plaster-of-paris mould, building section by section until he had created an interlocking igloo which when assembled covered every surface of the original sculpture it housed.

When satisfied, Thomas sealed and strapped the empty mould together and poured in a molten wax and turpentine mixture. After leaving it to set, he reopened the mould and took out the copy.

Now, all Bill had to do was paint the wax model with a procelain slick, thin coat on top of thin coat to avoid causing air bubbles.

"We'll put that to dry now and have a cup of tea," decided Bill. They walked across the foundry, sidestepping the week's production that littered the floor, to the little office where Bill put on the kettle.

"Who's it going to be for when it's finished? Eric?"

"No," replied Thomas, "Pamela Corran has commissioned it for her father's birthday. I wish it had been for Eric."

"Mm, I don't like Corran either," said Bill. "Did you see his photo in one of the colour supplements?"

"No," answered Thomas. "When was that?"

"I'm not sure. I saw it yesterday." Bill replied, searching a cluttered table for it. "It was here. Someone must have had it. There were two photos of him. One with his arm around Miss World and another of him sharing a joke with some big knob at a shindig he threw at the New Ritz."

Thomas didn't let on that he had been there as well.

"That man is just full of PR clichés. Don't worry if you can't find it," Thomas told Bill.

It was typical, he thought, for Corran to be photographed with beautiful women – all part and parcel of promoting cosmetics – but he would have liked to have seen the colour supplement. He was curious to see who Corran had put up in a bid to gain respectability and credibility.

"Sorry Tom, it must have been thrown," said Bill as he poured the tea. With their mugs in their hands they strolled back to the foundry floor.

For half an hour Bill was occupied with packing the porcelained wax model carefully into a boxed mixture of oil and fine casting sand, leaving just one inlet and an outlet for the molten bronze to be poured. But first it had to be put into a kiln to bake all the moisture out of it. This was necessary because if moisture had been retained, an explosion would occur when it came into contact with the hot metal.

"Come back tomorrow, we'll have a go at it at about dinner time," said Bill, securing the oven. "There's nothing more we can do today."

Thomas thought that, with time left on his hands, he would visit Mrs Evans in hospital. On the way he bought her a huge bouquet of carnations, hoping she'd be well enough to see them. As soon as he entered the ward he saw her, bolstered up by starched white pillows. In spite of the trauma she'd suffered, she looked her usual jolly self, unruffled, in contrast to her drawn, tired son sitting at the bedside. She greeted Thomas with mimed enthusiasm having to rest her scorched throat.

Presenting her with the flowers, Thomas found a chair and sat next to Jed, saving Mrs Evans from having to turn her head as he guessed that this movement would hurt her throat and chest. Deaf, and now temporarily dumb, she couldn't join the conversation, mimed or otherwise.

"You don't know if they've had any luck with the fingerprints on the bottle do you?" Jed unhesitatingly asked him.

"No, I haven't seen anything," Thomas bluffed, not knowing what bottle Jed was talking about. Another case of the uniformed officer being kept uninformed! Jed unknowingly helped him out of his embarrassment.

"Funny how that one should have been taken but, there you are, in a panic the thief probably grabbed what he could and dropped or chucked what he thought was useless. He probably wanted to lighten his load, as it doesn't look as if he had a get-away car."

"That sounds like what happened," said Thomas beginning to pick up the gist of the story. "I didn't actually see the bottle myself. Was it big?" he asked.

"No, not particularly – just 10ml of Buscopan Compositum." Jed was desperately trying to search his memory, "obviously of no use to the thief. The bloody problem is, I can't for the life of me remember if I'd put it in the drugs cabinet or if I'd left it stacked with the packed ones behind the door. I may have put the odd bottle in the cabinet. I don't know, the fire destroyed so much. There was no reason for them to be under lock and key."

"Perhaps you'll remember when you're under less strain," Thomas said sympathetically. "What is Buscopan used for anyway?"

"It's a smooth-muscle relaxant for horses, very effective in the treatment of colic, my first choice every time. In fact it works by slowing down the gut movement, allowing it to return to normal."

"Could a layman give it to a horse?" Thomas asked.

"He could if he knew how to give an injection, but it should only be administered by a veterinary surgeon because, if the doses have to be repeated, then there is the possibility of gut impaction, which is the complete seizure of the guts. If this happened then the horse would die," Jed explained.

"Does this Buscopan contain anything that a druggy could make use of?" Thomas asked.

"You tell me. There is painkiller in it. It's 4 mg of Hyoscine N-butyl-bromide and 500 mg of Dipsyrone."

The expression on Thomas's face showed that he was lost – these drugs weren't in his vocabulary. Mumbling he said, "I suppose a druggy will try anything as a substitute, when he can't get the real thing," then more positively he offered, "I'll have to refer to the drugs department to know whether it would be possible for this to be used. The chemicals you've named mean nothing to me. As you say, he probably blindly grabbed what he could and dropped that bottle during his escape."

Thomas's voice trailed off as his eye caught a headline on one of the newspapers left on the trolley at the foot of Mrs Evans's bed. It read, 'Eyecatcher Death Scare Threatens the Arc'.

Mrs Evans saw Thomas looking at the pile of dailies she had saved and beckoned him to have a closer study. She was tickled pink to see her photograph in so many and was going to keep a scrapbook about the fire when she was out of hospital. Thomas took up the invitation, pretending to take an interest in the fire reports, but instead used the opportunity to turn the pages to the Eyecatcher story. He read:

> "We can exclusively report that Eyecatcher, the housewives' choice and odds-on favourite for the Prix de l'Arc de Triomphe, has been the subject of death threats. During an interview at Newmarket races, trainer Eric Best confirmed that the unbeaten racehorse was being given specialist security treatment. This, as a result of a number of death threat telephone calls received at the Eagle Lodge stables."

Best was quoted saying that he was unable to reveal any more details but that in the light of the Shergar incident he felt that any such threats would have to be treated seriously, especially with such a valuable horse at stake. The report went on to say that a French professional security team had been consulted who specialized in racehorse protection and Best added that he had every confidence in the team's ability to see the horse safely through his trip abroad. When asked if the police had been informed of the threats, Best's reply was that consideration had been made as to whether or not to consult the police, but that Thatchit Corran, the owner of the horse, had said that he was entirely satisfied with the present arrangements and that, as no further threats had been forthcoming, felt there was no need to engage police assistance at this stage.

The rest of the report was just background on Eyecatcher's career.

'That reminds me,' Thomas thought, 'I've got to

get in touch with Summer about the tickets for France.' He folded the papers neatly and replaced them on the bed trolley. Getting to his feet, Thomas gently held Mrs Evans's hand and gave her a few encouraging words. She looked up and smiled gratefully at him, mouthing, "Thank you for coming." He said goodbye and left.

As soon as he got home he was on the telephone to Summer.

"Where have you been?" she said, as if desperate to talk to him, "I've been telephoning you all day trying to catch you."

"Sorry, Summer," he said, "I've been sorting out the casting today, then I went to see Mrs Evans, you know Jed the vet's mother, the one that was in that fire."

"Yes, that was terrible," Summer said, "How is she?"

"Bit sore, but she'll pull through," Thomas replied.

"A hell of a lot's happened in the last few days, Thomas," Summer said, sounding upset.

"What's up?"

"For a start, I've got your ticket for Paris, but I won't be joining you."

"Why not?" Thomas said, hoping he'd be able to change her mind.

"The sod has taken Eyecatcher there already," she started to cry, "and left me in charge here. I was so looking forward to going."

"Why so sudden?" Thomas said, disappointed himself.

In between sniffs, she told him, "I think they panicked a bit after that press release. One minute

Eric said that they were going out early to give the horse a chance to get over his journey, the next minute he was saying that they were putting him in hiding at a stable about 20 miles from Paris until the Arc. That's why Jed Evans was up here so late on the night of the fire. He had to rush the health certificate through, certifying Eyecatcher fit to run in France."

"Has Eric gone then?" he asked.

"Yes, but there was a blazing row here the morning after the fire between Ravir and him. I thought they were going to start fighting. It seems Ravir has some hold over Eric at the moment, but whatever was going on between them, they've gone with the horse and left me here to look after the place."

"You mean you're staying there at night as well?" Thomas said.

"Yes," she said, "I'm absolutely raving. He can stuff his job when he gets back. Please come over and cheer me up."

"Where's Adam?" Thomas asked.

"Oh, he's all sorted out," she replied, "he's at my mother's."

"OK, give me half an hour and I'll be with you. Do you fancy a meal?"

"Sounds nice," Summer answered, a little happier, "but I haven't got much to change into. Can we go scruffy?"

"Yeh, scruffy it is," Thomas said. "See you in half an hour."

In less than that he arrived at the stables. She met him in the yard, wearing jeans and leather jacket, ready to go.

"What about the horses?" he asked.

"Oh, they'll be alright. They've been fed and watered, got their blankets on. They're probably sleeping now."

Thomas took her to a little Greek restaurant, where jeans didn't matter and the food was always superb.

Thomas ordered lamb for both of them and picked up the conversation about the Arc.

"As the race isn't until a week tomorrow, what's happening to all his runners for next week?"

"There were only five," Summer said, "but I think Eric's withdrawn them all. Here are your tickets," she said, handing Thomas an envelope. "I've booked you for next Wednesday, I hope that's alright. You're in the Hotel Royal in Paris, it's very pricey but they've put on a special package deal for the Arc. It was difficult to find anywhere, everything's booked up. So that's all your winnings gone, but you can charge it to Miss Corran."

"Hey, come on now," Thomas said, reaching over for her hand. "It's not like you to be bitchy."

"I'm sorry," she said, "but I was so looking forward to it."

"Listen," he said, looking into her eyes. "We wouldn't have been able to see much of each other anyway, with you racing. Why don't I stay in Paris and you come and join me after the Arc when Eric gets back."

A smile lit up Summer's face. Thomas had said the right thing.

CHAPTER FIFTEEN

The next day Thomas was back at the foundry. Being Sunday, only Bill and another foundryman were working. They were there solely to cast his sculpture and when he arrived they were already pouring the molten bronze with expert skill. They instinctively knew how hot it should be. Too cold and it would solidify before running into the little channels, such as the ears. Too hot and the heavier masses such as the body and flanks, would bubble and become pitted. This was the lost wax method, so called because when the bronze was introduced into the mould it would instantly vapourize the wax and burn off any residue. They then had to wait anxiously through the cooling process before the birth of the finished piece like expectant fathers, praying for ten fingers and ten toes.

It took four games of cards and three mugs of tea before the result was known. The sand, now baked hard and crusty, was knocked away and the bronze quickly dowsed in water. When the steam subsided and the cast was cool enough to handle, Bill wire-brushed it for Thomas to examine scrupulously. A success! a perfect cast! Thomas was over the moon. The foundrymen, proud of their work, shared in the celebrations and joined him in the pub for a few pints before going home for dinner.

At home, Thomas sat with the sculpture on his lap and marked the places he would have to clean up and work on to obtain the perfect finish. He'd have to be very careful for it was surprising how soft bronze was when attacked with a small hammer and chisel. Then all that would be left would be to treat it with chemicals to precipitate the colours to the surface until he acquired the desired shades before finally comparing it with Eyecatcher. Feeling the weight of it in his hands, although it was hollow, caused him to hope it wouldn't be too heavy for hand luggage on the aircraft. He'd have to check.

CHAPTER SIXTEEN

On Monday, after parade, Thomas went straight to the sergeant's office to arrange his time off. With 12 days overtime on his card, and with house-to-house enquiries completed, the force was keen to give him the time off to add to his four-day winter leave rather than let him claim payment.

The next stop was CID.

"Any luck, with the bottle?" he asked DC Gardener.

"What bottle?" Tim asked.

"You know," Thomas said, impatiently, "the Buscopan found outside the scene of the fire."

"Oh, that," he said, now understanding. "There's a print on it. A definite little finger I believe. All we need now is a name to go with it."

Fingerprint searches at Scotland Yard were more simplified if suspect's names were put forward and, provided they were on record, the prints could be compared with the one found at the scene almost immediately. But without a name thousands of prints had to be searched for a match, a laborious painstaking exercise only afforded to major crimes and a result could take anything up to a month.

"Any suggestions to offer?" Tim asked.

"No, unfortunately," said Thomas. "It was just that Jed Evans was enquiring. If I do get something I'll let you know."

"Hey, would you like me to put a word in? I could get you in on the case if you liked."

"No thanks," said Thomas, "I'm off to Paris for a couple of weeks."

The drugs department was next. The decor here reflected the subject matter of the job. Potted plant exhibits flourished on the window sills, awaiting court cases. Pipes, photographs and souvenirs of successful raids festooned the walls.

Two earringed officers sat at their desks. Both looked like unkempt hippies, probably chosen because of the easy way they adapted themselves to that appearance.

One stopped typing as he entered the room, the other was on the telephone.

"What can we do for you, man?" he asked Thomas.

"Buscopan," Thomas began, but before he had to struggle further with the names, the drugs officer stopped him.

"Hyoscine N-butyl-bromide and Dipsyrone. Forget it, a druggy would only be interested in that combination if he wanted to commit suicide. We did a check on it for the incident room. They were given the report this morning."

"Oh! Right," said Thomas, impressed, "you're on the ball. Have you got any ideas as to who it could be?"

"We're watching a few faces but there's no word on the street. It's a bit early yet."

"OK," said Thomas, "see you."

"Yeh man, anytime. Stay cool," he replied and carried on typing. Although he worked in the same station, Thomas never failed to be intrigued by the guises and attitudes each department brought out in the people who worked in them. He wondered if he would talk like that in time if he dressed like a hippy.

CHAPTER SEVENTEEN

Wednesday came quicker than Thomas would have liked. It was 11am and he was packed and ready to fly. He had spent the last thirty minutes speaking to his wife on the telephone. True to form, she had found the most awkward time to approach him on a serious subject.

"Thomas, I think if you give me a chance, everything will be OK between us." She explained that her ex-husband had suddenly decided to marry someone else. The way seemed open for Cathy to have custody of her boy.

"Look love, I can't stop now," Thomas tried to explain, "but by all means bring him home. I'm sure we'll get on. I'll be away for a few days but I'll see you when I get back, then we can discuss the matter properly."

Putting the phone down he hadn't fully taken in the promised change in lifestyle a live-in wife would bring him, although, he thought, a child at home would be nice.

The flight to Paris was quick, efficient and pleasant for Thomas. He had been allowed to take his sculpture as hand-luggage and upon arrival had found no difficulty in locating the hotel. He was also pleased with his room, the telephone and shower – essential to his relaxation.

Thomas switched on the television and watched as he unpacked. He hadn't realised until the sound came on that it was going to be in French. He tried to listen for the odd recognizable word but the French newscaster was speaking so fast he couldn't understand a thing she was saying. After the news there seemed to be a sports item. He caught 'Longchamp' and 'Prix de l'Arc de Triomphe'. Then he saw the horse being unloaded off the plane. The picture changed and he heard the words, 'Eyecatcher' and 'Entraîneur Monsieur Eric Best', as the horse was seen doing a small half-canter, watched by Eric with the host-trainer of the stable where he was lodging and the interviewer. Thomas couldn't make head or tail of the rest of the dialogue and resigned himself to the fact that he'd have to try and obtain an English newspaper to bring him up to date. Betting prices flashed on the screen. Eyecatcher was an expected 4 to 1 on, four thousand pounds to win one thousand and stake returned. What a risk he thought! No wonder it was described as the sport of kings.

A short walk from the hotel he found a newsstand with plenty of papers and soon established that Eyecatcher was being housed at Chantilly, forty-three kilometres north of Paris in stables run by Paul Bouvac. All was going well for the big day and a press conference was planned for the morning. Thomas intended to attend. This would be his last chance, other than the race itself to compare his sculpture with the live animal.

*   *   *

Hiring a car and taking what directions he could, he took to the Paris streets. It didn't take long to appreciate that French drivers knew only two speeds – fast and stop, while the state of his hired car indicated that bumpers in France were meant for bumping.

When he eventually found his way out of Paris and reached Chantilly, Thomas was in a cold sweat, not from driving on the wrong side of the road – he'd soon adjusted to that – but from getting lost in traffic that forced and dictated his pace with ever-impatient tactics. Looking for help was hopeless. He saw it was the same in France – you could never find a policeman when you wanted one.

The morning was crisp and bright. 'Thank God' he thought, 'I didn't have to drive in fog'. A throng of reporters and cameramen were at the gallops watching Eyecatcher going through his paces, so Thomas took up a position which presented him with a good view out of a direct line with Eric. After Summer's disappointment he wanted to avoid him. Eyecatcher galloped past with a pacemaker and Thomas's stomach dropped. He couldn't explain what was wrong but the sculpture was not a good likeness at all. Thomas wondered if the flight had taken its toll out of the horse but thought it more likely that he'd made the mistake of relying too heavily on Summer's photographs which had been taken when the horse was a year younger. Perhaps the cast had shrunk, something he'd never experienced before. But he didn't even know if this was feasible – all he could be sure of was that he had created a poor likeness.

Perplexed and feeling very disappointed, he made

himself scarce and drove back to the hotel. He lay on the bed with the sculpture in front of him, finding it hard to accept it was wrong, drank a bottle of wine and fell asleep.

At 5pm he woke and decided he must telephone Summer. Getting connected was no problem and he was amazed at the quality of the line.

"Thomas?" she said, surprised to hear him sounding so close. "Where are you?"

"In my hotel room," he replied, dejectedly.

"You don't sound so good. What's wrong?"

"It's the bronze – there's something wrong and I can't put my finger on it."

"You're too much of a perfectionist, that's your trouble," she said. "Surely the cast wouldn't alter from the sculpture you did and, from what I saw of that, it was excellent. Anybody could see it was Eyecatcher straight off."

"Not now, they couldn't," he replied, far from being consoled. "I just can't understand it – I know it's far fetched but I'm almost positive that there's been a switch. There can't be any other explanation for it."

The surprise caused Summer to pause before commenting, "To start with – are you sure you were looking at the right horse?"

"Positive," he answered. "I went to the press conference at Chantilly. I mean, everybody else thought it was the right horse. It was the only one there, except for a pacemaker who was a chestnut with a white blaze. They were all taking photographs and filming him. It had to be Eyecatcher, otherwise what was the point."

"All I can think of," Summer suggested, "is that

Corran and Ravir have done a swop to protect Eye-catcher from being assassinated."

"That's a bit of a cheek," Thomas said, "although without the sculpture I wouldn't have been able to spot any difference myself. But where has this double come from?" he asked.

"Could be one of Paul's," Summer replied. "I can't see them getting away with taking two identical-looking horses over to France. If the punters were to get a smell of it they'd cry fix."

"That's what's puzzling me," said Thomas. "I can't see anyone going to all that trouble to find a look-a-like for Eyecatcher just for the benefit of a press conference. Why didn't they just hold off and not give one?"

"You think that Eric and Corran are intending to run a ringer, substituting Eyecatcher in the Arc then?" Summer asked, not fully convinced herself.

"I know it sounds far fetched, Summer. I've turned it over and over in my mind searching for a motive but that's what I suspect."

"Thomas, you know as well as I do there's not a horse in the world to touch him. Why put a ringer in?" Summer said, trying to be realistic.

"Well, what if Eyecatcher had colic – perhaps they could put the ringer in, hoping to save the bets." Thomas was thinking aloud.

"That's nonsense and well you know it. We're talking about the richest race in Europe after all. If a ringer were to stand a chance of getting placed in it, he'd have to be top class and, take it from me, there aren't any ringers of that quality about."

"What about Sparrow Hawk?" he suggested.

"Sparrow Hawk!" she raised her tone in disbelief.

"He's only a handicapper – wouldn't stand a cat in hell's chance against an Arc field."

"Well, what if they were planning for Eyecatcher to lose so that they could have a big bet on the second best horse in the race or even a dark horse at a big price."

"That's more feasible," Summer conceded, "but a bit risky. They'd have to be pretty sure about the horse that was carrying their money and I don't know if they'd get away with it. A dismal performance by Eyecatcher would draw the attention of the stewards. That's how most ringers are detected, not by some clever official checking its passport, but by an incredible performance being put up in conjunction with abnormal betting activity. No, sorry, Thomas, I can't buy that either. Any more ideas?'

"No," Thomas said, "I'm dry on ideas. I was hoping you might have the answer. Just to satisfy me, will you check if Sparrow Hawk is in fact Sparrow Hawk and not Eyecatcher?"

"You're out of luck," Summer answered. "I can't because he's not here. He's been sent somewhere to school over the jumps."

"When is he due back?" Thomas asked curiously.

"I'm not sure – could be sometime this week. Eric was a bit vague on that – told me not to worry, saying arrangements had been made to return him when his schooling was over. It shouldn't take long though – he's jumped before. It was only a refresher to get him to stand off his fences. Eric couldn't fit it in himself, what with being away this week, and I think he's got a National Hunt buyer for him. Listen," she said as she searched for a way of helping him, "if you're really serious about this, then there's one sure-fire way of finding out if the horse is Eyecatcher or not and that's to try that perfume on him. You did remember to get me some duty free, I hope."

"Yeah, I got you some," Thomas said, "but fat chance I've got of getting close enough for him to smell it. What's he supposed to do anyhow when he does get a whiff?"

Summer laughed. "First he'll give a little whinny and curl up his muzzle the same way Cliff Richard curls up his top lip, then you just stand back and watch how things develop. Oh, and make sure you've got your legs crossed."

"Very funny," he said, laughing in spite of himself. "I'll have a go. When do you plan on coming over?"

"It'll have to be after the race, when Eric gets back – probably next Monday afternoon. By the way, don't try phoning me tomorrow or Saturday. I'm supposed to take a two-year-old up to Hamilton. Eric faxed me with last minute instructions this morning. He forgot to take her out of the race and, with the going being heavy, she's in with a good chance. Not many suitable races left for her this season. It will mean that I've got to travel up tomorrow night that's all, ready for Saturday. Eric said he'd sort out the feeding et cetera with someone else. So don't waste your money trying to get me until I'm back on Sunday morning. Hey, this call must be costing you a fortune. Here's a big kiss."

"Big kiss back," Thomas said. "Wet dreams."

CHAPTER EIGHTEEN

Thunderstorms and continuous heavy rain covered Scotland and the North of England that night and there was no sign of it abating the following day. Summer telephoned the course before setting off to be told that the meeting was to be abandoned. She relaxed. It was the news she had been half hoping to hear.

Sitting in the hotel lounge, Thomas experienced the comforting change of conversations blending from French to English as the hotel began to fill with race trippers. It was 8pm and he'd chosen an empty table but the seats around him were inevitably going to be filled. Two couples were hovering dangerously close. They were in their early sixties and it appeared that one of the ladies was choosing Thomas's table for them all. The ladies were elegantly dressed, determined to air their summer outfits for one last annual occasion. The men were in light suits.

"Are these seats taken?"

Thomas would have liked to have said yes, but resigned himself to a no. Drinks in hand, they took their seats and invaded his world but excluded him from their conversation.

"Such a shame, Eyecatcher's been withdrawn

from the Arc," one of the ladies said to the other, disappointedly. "That's all George and I came over for – to see him race."

"Does anyone know why?" one of the men asked, in a plummy voice and an air which suggested that he felt he should have been consulted first.

"*Colic,*" the other said. "Bloody thing's got *colic.* No guts that Best fellow – afraid to lose."

Thomas couldn't believe it, didn't want to believe it. He'd only just finished building his own theories to convince himself that the horse he'd seen wasn't Eyecatcher. This news shattered them all, leaving him again totally perplexed. Now he was faced with the daunting prospect of having to sculpt Eyecatcher all over again.

With a face resembling the way he was feeling he sank back into his plush French grey chair, not in the mood for mixing with strangers.

God! Right now all he wanted was a night out on the town with the boys. He could sense, especially from the women, that they wanted to involve him rather than have him listening in. Now and again, at the end of a statement, one would look across at him, inviting a comment. Thomas tried deliberately to resist although he was feeling uneasy, as if he were intruding even though it had been his table originally. It was just that he didn't want to join in the usual repartee he'd learnt to expect from people when they were introduced to an off-duty policeman, and the fact that he was without jurisdiction in Paris wouldn't make a ha'pence of difference.

He could see it now. The set pieces were "Oh! I've got a nephew in the police force. Do you know him?" He never did know them. They were always in a different force and people just couldn't appreciate the unlikelihood of him knowing their relative. This usually had the embarrassing effect of a conversation stopper. The other old chestnut was "Tell, me, how much are you allowed to drink before you fail the breathaliser?"

But this time, without knowing his profession, the opening line was, "Are you over for the race?"

"Yes, I am," replied Thomas, sitting up for the sake of good manners, "and, in fact, if what you say is true I share in your disappointment over Eyecatcher. I've been commissioned to do a bronze of him and I must say that this news has come as a shock."

"Oh! How interesting. Frank, this man is a sculptor," the woman said to the man with a plummy voice. Frank! He didn't look like a Frank. Thomas would have put him more as a Nigel or an Edward – he was usually good at guessing names but his judgement seemed to be impaired all round these last couple of weeks.

"Were you to sculpt him winning the Arc?" said Frank.

"No," answered Thomas. "I've already completed the sculpture. I only came over to Paris to do the final touches, but to hear that he's been taken out of the race leaves me deeply disappointed." The woman sympathised with him. Frank raised a hand to attract a waiter's attention – he wanted to buy a round of drinks.

"I'd very much like to see it when it's finished. Can I get you a refill?"

"Thank you," said Thomas, pleased to be introduced into a round. "I'll have the same again, please. Brandy."

As Frank gave his order the other woman took up the conversation. "Our daughter used to do a bit of eventing, only her 'old Freddy' is too old now. I'm sure she'd love a bronze of him before he dies." Her husband nodded in agreement. "Would you be able to do one of him?"

"I'll have a go," Thomas offered.

"How will we get in touch?" she asked.

"Here," Thomas said, writing down his name and address and telephone number. He handed it to the woman as Frank took the drinks off the tray and tipped the waiter.

"Oh!" she said, surprised to read the English address. "I would have said you were Welsh."

"I was born in Wales. In fact my parents still live there, but I haven't for more than ten years," explained Thomas.

"You still have a trace of that nice sing-song Welsh accent. We've always wanted to go to Wales, haven't we dear," she said, turning to her husband. "Is it as quaint as you see in the films? I mean, it's not a million miles away but I've never been there in my life – nor Scotland for that matter. Have you two been to Wales?" she asked the other couple.

"No," Frank's wife answered. "We're from Kent," as if that explained everything.

Without formal introductions they still slowly got to know one another. They accepted that he was a sculptor and didn't dig deeper. Relaxed and with the rounds coming around quite quickly, he was happy to tell them about his beautiful Wales, wholeheartedly describing and recommending many of the

South West coastal villages and resorts, ". . . and then you must try Tenby, it has three beaches and the best weather in Wales." As the evening progressed, Frank, Mary, Stephanie and George were sold on Wales and trying to make a decision as to whether it would be the Gower coast or the Pembrokeshire coast for their next holidays.

"Go to them all," Thomas said, now half-cut. "There's only about seventy miles between the lot of them." That settled, the talk turned to racing, food, anything and everything. The atmosphere was good and everybody was getting too drunk on brandy, port and wine to be affected by the news of Eye-catcher which had originally depressed them.

The party eventually broke up with the promise to meet the following night for a game of Trivial Pursuits with a difference – where getting an answer right would mean knocking back your drink.

Legless, he wasn't aware of getting to his room, but by 3am he was soundly asleep and nothing was likely to wake him up. His head had finally come to rest where he had laid it after observing the room spinning around at vomit-provoking speeds!

Summer's slumber was not alcohol-induced. She was a light sleeper and the surroundings of Eagle Lodge, with its peculiar noises and unfamiliar sounds, had frequently brought her to consciousness every night she had stayed there. The equine lodgers had seen to that, kicking over the odd bucket, rubbing an itchy neck on the stable door or kicking to move an uncomfortable blanket – this was all sparsely laced with noises made by the cockerel. Friendly, though disturbing, the sounds contrasted strongly with those of her little home, where the creaking of central heating pipes or a sigh from the dog wouldn't register as a signal for her to wake up. Summer wasn't usually the nervous, imaginative sort but she did like her own bed.

It wasn't long before she was lying with her eyes open, fully aware that the noise she could now hear was totally out of place for the time of night. The banging and clattering of hooves as they scurried down a horse box ramp or the loud welcoming whinny from the residents – she wasn't sure which of these had awakened her, warning her of the strange activity in the yard.

With only Meg the sheepdog for company, Summer looked out of the bedroom window which conveniently offered the best view of most of the stables. Looking down into the yard, she could see nothing that could explain the disturbance, nothing that would settle her mind and allow her to return to bed.

In between the short periods when it was eclipsed by the passing clouds, the full moon illuminated the yard and it appeared the animals had returned to their slumber. Summer decided to venture outside and check, hoping Meg would be close at hand.

As she pulled on her jodhpurs, the sudden unmistakable sound of a diesel lorry starting up confirmed that there was someone in the yard. The sweeping headlights of the lorry illuminated her room in a stroke as it turned around in one manoeuvre. Struggling to get back to the window, with her jodhpurs restrictingly only half on, Summer was just in time to see a horse transporter drive away, its red tail-lights disappearing in the darkness.

Now fully dressed and armed with a long powerful

hand-torch, Summer felt a little braver. If somebody had just stolen a horse, then they had left. She had to investigate which one, if any, had been taken. Thinking of telephoning the police, she suddenly realised, walking downstairs, that nothing more sinister had happened than the return of Sparrow Hawk. Of course, Eric wouldn't have known that the Hamilton meeting had been abandoned and whoever had just deposited the horse wouldn't have expected a reception. Relieved and glad that she hadn't made a fool of herself by calling the police, Summer opened the door to the chill night air. All was quiet, too quiet. She looked across to the fillies, her senses telling her that someone was still present, someone remaining in the dark shadows. She tried to push the feeling to the back of her mind and steeled herself, determined not to be frightened. Meg came from somewhere and joined her, prancing in front, excited by the novelty of a middle-of-the-night walk. Summer became less tense in her company and systematically began to check every stable.

Starting with the fillies she found them edgy, on their toes. Something was bothering them but this wasn't unusual. A cat, rat or perhaps an owl – any little harmless presence could set them off with their infectious worry. Soothing each one in turn with comforting talk Summer counted them all. As she moved across to the other inmates her loneliness disappeared. She would have felt happier dossing down in some hay with one of the horses than having to return to the empty house. She'd left the door off the latch and feared now that someone could have entered in her absence.

Checking the other horses, she found these present

and correct but, unlike the fillies, the geldings and colts were unperturbed, either sleeping or munching softly at their hay.

Right! Where has Sparrow Hawk been put, she thought? His box was empty. Summer resigned herself to the fact that she would have to check the only remaining boxes which were near the offices and covered-school where Eyecatcher had been recently housed. This section was overshadowed by the house and looked a lot less inviting than the moonlit yard she was leaving. Each step she took across the gravel was more forbidding than the last. Meg was no longer in front of her. Summer looked around and could see her hanging back. She called to her but the sheepdog coyly refused the invitation to join her and just stood wagging her tail.

Summer approached Eyecatcher's box, finding it closed and padlocked. Eric or Ravir had the key, ensuring that the box stayed clean with its newly laid straw bed to await the hero's return. She flashed the torch and it glinted on the base of the padlock, highlighting an inserted key. Looking closer she saw that the key had already been used to open the padlock which was still in position in the bolt. A small whinny sounded from the covered-school about fifty yards down wind. Turning quickly, she shone the torch in that direction. Unmistakably there was a horse there, tethered to the entrance. He was pawing the ground impatiently. Summer walked nervously towards the horse, concerned for his well-being in the cold night but shaking with fear, knowing she had disturbed someone, someone who's intention had been to leave the horse tied while the door was unlocked, someone who she'd felt was about from the moment she'd stepped outside, someone who worried the fillies, someone Meg didn't want to meet.

Summer's knuckles were white with the grip she had on the torch and, as she ventured forward, tears started to fill her eyes. She was a lot closer now as the horse gave out a squeal, his muzzle turned up into the Cliff Richard curl, in reaction to Summer's perfume.

"Eyecatcher!" she said in amazement, "What on earth . . ."

Shocked and not quite knowing what to do next, she untied him. Leading him away from where she sensed the danger lurked she couldn't resist looking behind her, shining the torch beyond the entrance into the far end of the covered-school. Freezing on the spot she saw the white Porsche. Standing next to it in what had been complete blackness was Ravir. He'd been waiting, holding a stiletto knife in his hand. Not able to shout nor able to run Summer impulsively mounted Eyecatcher who instantly galvanized into action, causing her to lose the reins. He was already across the lawned paddock and heading for the lane at the main entrance when the headlights of the Porsche began the chase. Screeching and snaking on the loose surface of the school Ravir soon had the car under control and in immediate pursuit. Squeezing with her legs, holding on for dear life, Summer only wanted to stay in front, to get away, anywhere safe. Without steering nor direction Eyecatcher decided to head for the main road, almost losing his footing on the turn but, although riding bareback, Summer was well balanced now and able to stay with him. If the horse could get her across the road before the Porsche caught up then she'd be safe in the fields leading to woodland where no car could follow. Failing this she desperately needed a saving stranger to be driving in the area. Eyecatcher was galloping on the grass verge of the lane. Summer was thankful for that – to do the same on the hard lane surface would have injured the horse's legs.

The tanker driver drove steadily along the main road, panel lights illuminating his cab in red, orange and blue. The heater was at a luxurious setting and, in shirt sleeves, he sang along to the radio tuned to a music station. With the road ahead open and traffic free, the tachograph recorded a speed of 60 mph.

Eyecatcher saw the lorry at the same time as Summer, stopping with hoof-ripping suddeness. The effectiveness of his reflexes took advantage of Summer's precarious seat, the momentum ejecting her like a rag doll across the path of the unsuspecting lorry driver. The windscreen smashed at the instant of impact, crazing into a blinding whiteness. Fighting for control of the lorry as he hit the brakes, he caught the first hint of explanation – out of the corner of his eye he saw a racehorse!

Bringing the eight tonner to a stop he left the cab, running back to the scene. The Porsche rocketed out of the lane screeching to hold the road. As it sped off, the lorry driver dived out of the way to avoid it. Scrambling back to his feet he ran to his cab for a torch, switching it on to show his existence, and ran back to the lane junction. He could hear Eyecatcher's hooves fading in the distance.

It didn't take the driver long to find Summer's body on the road. He knelt over her and gently cleared the blood-matted hair from her face; already there was a spreading pool circling her head. Carefully, he turned her onto her side, hoping to find a way to stop the bleeding, his hands soaked in warm blood which dried stickily between his fingers. Shining the torch he saw the causes of the bleeding, the gorey mess, the hole where there should have been an ear.

In sheer panic, he looked around for help. Seeing the lights of Eagle Lodge up the lane he ran towards them, involuntarily vomitting as he kept reliving the vivid images which were repeating in his mind's eye. Shouting and banging on the door without response, he tried the handle and, finding it unlocked, went in and telephoned the police.

Richard Speak, observer in a traffic car, reached the scene as the lorry driver got back. The blue lights strobed the tragedy and an ambulance could be heard on its way. Caringly, Richard laid his warm coat over the still unconscious Summer, not sure if she was dead but afraid to damage her broken body by moving her. The bleeding had stopped. The other policeman urgently radioed for the scene-of-crime officer and further back-up to assist. A doctor was already on the way. "Can you tell me what happened?" Richard asked the driver, offering him the opportunity to sit in the back of the police car.

"I don't know," said the driver. "I can't explain it. I didn't even see what I'd hit until I found her. I thought it was a horse – I saw a horse."

Richard shone his torch on the road surface and found a horseshoe. He saw the tell-tale white iron scratches in the tar, the hoof marks in the grass. He didn't ponder over them – he was looking for Summer's ear.

"There was a car, a Porsche," the lorry driver said.

He was now out of the police car and following Richard around.

"– a white Porsche, too dark to see the number. I don't mind giving a breathaliser. I mean, I don't want there to be any doubt. I haven't been drinking."

"That won't be necessary," said Richard. "It would be easier though, if you were to accompany us to the station. We won't keep you for more than an hour, besides, you look like you could do with a cup of tea." Richard could see something caught between the shattered windscreen and a twisted wiper. From a distance it looked like a parking ticket. He moved closer to examine it and saw it was the severed ear.

Richard retrieved it and handed it to the doctor who was now in the back of the ambulance with Summer. "Is there any hope for her?" Richard asked. This time he wasn't merely enquiring – he really wanted to be told that there was a chance, that she'd live, but the reply was a forlorn shake of the head.

"Her breathing's very shallow. I think there could be brain damage."

Richard closed the door and thought of Thomas as the ambulance pulled away.

At 7am the full picture still wasn't clear. Vital parts of the jigsaw were missing. Eyecatcher, sound except for over-reach cuts to his fetlocks, had been recovered from a field and identified by other stable staff. They had been understandably shocked by the news that greeted them when they had arrived that morning. Richard, however, had decided to withhold the information from Corran and Best, asking the staff not to make contact while the inquiries continued.

CHAPTER NINETEEN

Richard now had the unenviable task of breaking the news to Thomas. He found an empty office, shut the door and rang the Hotel Royal, Paris. It wasn't until the call was answered that he realised he may have to communicate with a receptionist who couldn't speak English. He was in luck – she spoke English, albeit with an American accent. He asked for Thomas Cord's room.

"Connecting you now, Sir."

The telephone rang and rang.

"There doesn't seem to any reply, Sir. Will you hold?" the receptionist enquired.

But before Richard had time to answer, Thomas picked up the receiver, his head thumping from the sudden loud awakening. With his forehead resting on the cold door for relief he answered, "Hallo."

"Thomas, it's Richard."

"Richard, Richard?" Thomas repeated, the name not sinking in past the buzz and blurr of his hangover.

"Your mate, Richard, Richard Speak," he said impatiently.

"Oh! Richard," Thomas's brain came into focus. Now he was curious why he should be telephoning.

"Are you in France?"

"No," he said, his tone serious, "I'm afraid I've got bad news."

"Not Crown Court," Thomas replied.

He knew he had a big case in the near future, which would have to have precedence over two weeks in Paris.

"No, Thomas. God, this is hard. I'm so upset myself. I don't know how you're going to take it."

Richard, trying to keep emotion out of his voice, was speaking clearly, aware of the importance of avoiding a misunderstanding.

"There's been an accident."

Thomas's mind frantically searched every corner of his brain for who it could be, who he least wanted it to be. He already feared the worst, that someone he loved had been killed.

As if detached from his body he heard himself say, "That's all right mate, I'm ready."

"It's Summer," Richard said. "Summer's been knocked down. I don't think she'll pull through." There was total silence on the other side. Richard felt helpless, wishing he knew how his friend had taken it. He said, "Thomas, are you OK?"

"Yes," he said softly, clearing his throat. "How did it happen?" Then in disbelief, "Come on, she's not that bad, you're just saying the worst, right?"

Richard repeated, "Thomas, I know this is hard, but make no mistake – she's very bad. The doctors don't hold out much hope." He outlined the injuries to Thomas followed by the facts surrounding the accident, but Thomas knew more than Richard. Urgently, yet with cold professionalism he said, "I'm leaving straight away. Check with a 'Hollywood Car

Hire'. They're a firm in London. A Serge Ravir has rented a Porsche of theirs. Get his details and do a full criminal records check on him. He's French. There might be nothing in Britain, but check with Interpol. Oh! and put him forward for the fingerprints at the vet's fire. What time is it now?"

"I make it five to eight," replied Richard.

"OK, I'll check with the airport and try to get a flight this morning. I'll ring you when I land. Perhaps you'll be able to pick me up?"

"Right," said Richard. "See you later."

Taking charge of himself, Thomas got to work and was on a plane within two hours.

On the flight home the memories of Summer flooded back. Thomas tried to hide in those memories rather than bring himself to face the truth that he might never see her again. That thought was making him feel strangely lonely.

He remembered how they had first met one Sunday morning at the police station. He had been married fifteen months, the first twelve to Cath, the remaining three to an empty bed. Summer had not long started at Eagle Lodge.

"Will somebody see to the desk?" the station officer had shouted down the corridor. "It's bloody hectic here – I've got three telephones ringing. Don't all rush at once will you."

Nobody volunteered but Thomas, being the closest, reluctantly walked down towards the reception hatch. When he saw Summer he was glad he had. Her perfume, her clothes, her hair! She wasn't wearing anything spectacular and her face was only lightly made-up but she was one of those girls who look good in whatever they wear. She knew what suited her and how to wear it to the best advantage. Her presence was captivating. Thomas had never been able to recall all she'd been wearing but remembered the high heeled boots and denims.

"I'm sorry to bother you," she'd said, "but I've lost my dog."

Thomas didn't care what she'd done – she was gorgeous. Their eyes had held each other longer than necessary.

Feeling awkward in the presence of such beauty, he reached above the hatch for the register and started to fill in the details of Summer's alsatian.

"His name is Buster," she offered.

"Oh, I don't need to know that. We shan't be interviewing him," Thomas joked.

She giggled attractively, lifting the back of her fingers to her mouth in an effort to stop. He couldn't help noticing her brilliant teeth and lovely eyes.

A tap on the shoulder turned his head.

"Can you manage?" It was the efficient station officer, now off the telephones.

"Yeh, sure," answered Thomas, "it's just a lost dog."

PC Phillips saw the reason for the delay and whistled approvingly out of ear shot. He filled in all the details, name, address, telephone number, description of dog, time, date and place lost, collar or no collar. The alsatian was there, the last entry, brought in only an hour previously. He closed the book and replaced it. Without telling Summer that her dog was already in the kennels at the back of the station, he assured her that he would personally see to it that everything that could be done to find Buster would be done.

"That's great," she said, full of hope. "Do you want me to sign anything?"

"No, that's OK," he said, taking a quick glance to make sure that there was no engagement ring on her finger. He'd already noticed from her details that she was a Miss. Feeling that there was nothing more she could say, Summer thanked him and turned away, leaving four heads at the hatch to watch her wiggle her way out.

"Cor! What a mover!" Richard had said, having arrived on the scene after the station officer had told him of the bit of crumpet at the desk. The other head, a probationer, had moved from the hatch and was gawking through a window overlooking the street, his eyes following her down the road.

PC Phillips had taken Thomas to one side and referred him to the entry detailing the alsatian which had already been brought in.

"The dog's here," he said.

"I know that," said Thomas, not believing the station constable could be so thick. "I'll take it up to her now. Give her a chance to get home first."

"You randy sod," Phillips said. "I hope he bites you."

Thomas hadn't thought of that and had spent the next fifteen minutes making friends with Buster, even giving him a pie from his own lunch-box.

The stewardess lent over and asked Thomas if he'd like something to drink.

He tried a gin and lemonade. He was thirsty, his mouth very dry, but the smell of the gin turned his stomach before it reached his lips.

"You don't have any headache tablets do you?" he asked. She fetched some and a glass of water.

"A barley sugar sometimes helps," she suggested and offered him one. He took it but his stomach churned, warning him not to put it in his mouth.

"Could I just try a black coffee?" he tentatively enquired. She nodded and fetched him one without hesitation, putting it on the little table at the back of the seat in front of him. The bit of attention slightly eased his head but the cold reality of Summer's accident remained. He drank the coffee and looked out of the window but there was no resistance against the heavy lids of his eyes closing. He drifted back to that first day.

Without giving anything else a chance to take priority, Thomas had put Buster into the back of a panda car and driven out of the station yard. He heard the sergeant's voice over his pocket radio.

"Where are you off to, Cord?" He was looking out of his office window at the panda, with dog, pulling away.

"Just returning a dog to its owner, Sarg," replied Thomas, not daring to stop for fear he'd have to return.

"Can't the owner pick it up then?" suggested the sergeant.

"Too heavy, Sergeant," he answered, regretting the sarcasm he had used.

"Very funny. Be back in ten minutes – I've got a job for you."

Thomas drove to Summer's house and put the promise of a bollocking from the sergeant to the back of his mind.

The pilot's voice over the intercom interrupted Thomas, pulling his thoughts back from reliving the past to the present. He was enjoying his memories and the interruption, whatever it was, wasn't strong enough to keep him from going back to their vivid images.

He remembered how Buster had been so full of excitement, enjoying the ride in preference to the isolation of the kennels he had just been released from and how he had stood with his hind legs on the back seat, indifferent to the dusty marks they were leaving as he settled with his front paws over the back of the front passenger seat, finally satisfied that he couldn't improve on the all-round unobstructed view. Thomas stopped the panda to try and persuade the alsatian to lie safely on the car floor, but it would have none of it and when he had realised that his attempts were futile he left the dog as it was.

He wasn't sure how the houses were numbered as he entered Summer's street. He parked the car, and decided to walk the dog on the police station lead to Summer's house which was number 22. Buster knew the house alright and had eagerly pulled Thomas towards it, his sudden strength jerking Thomas and causing his helmet to fall off. This boyish behaviour would have confused any passer-by who would have thought that Buster was an obedient, trained police dog. Pulling with both hands on the lead, Thomas had managed to slow the alsatian down to a fast walking pace as he dragged him to Summer's front door.

The dog had pushed his nose to the crack of the door and had whined as well as barked, his tail beating Thomas's leg until his mistress opened the door with delight, surprised to see Thomas at the other end of the lead.

"Buster!" she cried, and the dog leapt up at her,

knocking her off balance with his slobbering kisses. Thomas put out a hand to stop her falling. She accepted his help, and remarked, "That was quick, come in. Where did you find him?"

Thomas didn't know. He had forgotten to look in the dog register and said so.

"To be honest, I don't know. He was brought to the station when I wasn't there."

"Where've you been, you naughty boy?" she said to Buster with a half-hearted reprimand. The dog just barked and jumped up at Thomas, leaving an apron of hair over his uniform – the price of friendship, he thought.

"God, you're covered in hairs!" Summer said to him.

"That's the nicest thing anyone's ever said to me," Thomas replied. It got the desired response.

Summer laughed, "I meant your jacket's covered in hairs, not you. Take it off and I'll brush it for you." Thomas didn't hesitate, needing an excuse to stay while he thought of a way to ask her out. He handed his tunic over and she took it outside. He followed her to the door and watched as she brushed it, noticing her firm breasts jiggle under her white blouse at each stroke. He tried desperately to think of something original to say, but failed. Her beauty was blocking his thoughts and time was running out.

She handed him the tunic saying, "There, that's better," and Buster gave one bark.

"Oh, you must be starving," she said to the dog.

"I know a place where they do a nice doggy bag. I'll take you there tonight if you like," Thomas said in hope. Summer smiled.

"OK," she answered, "but I'll pay. After all, he's my dog."

"We'll see," Thomas said and arranged to pick her up at eight.

Summer's love for him had ignited almost spontaneously and with enough flame to rekindle Thomas's if it were ever to go out. It never had and it never would.

"'Bye Summer, I love you," he mouthed before drifting into a restful sleep.

The next thing he heard was the pilot announcing the landing. He was back.

Going through the green channel at customs he was stopped and approached for a random check. The customs officer went through his routine patter, carefully searching Thomas's baggage after confirming that he had nothing to declare. They were joined by another customs officer who showed an unhealthy interest in the sculpture. 'I hope I don't have to pay duty on that,' he thought.

"I took it out with me," he explained. "I made it," hoping that would be sufficient. He didn't want to draw his warrant card. That sometimes made matters worse. After having it x-rayed, the officers were still suspicious but returned it to him with the necessary clearance.

The answer to the whole mystery suddenly hit Thomas like a bolt out of the blue. Desperately, he telephoned the station to say he had landed and was ready to be picked up – a police car would be quicker than a taxi.

"Is Summer all right? Is there any news?"

Nobody seemed to know. The last they had heard was 'no change'. "What hospital is she at?" Nobody knew that either. "Ask Richard when he gets there – he's dealing with the case."

It was a waste of time asking anything else, so he said, "Transfer me to the drugs department." He was put through.

* * *

Richard picked him up twenty minutes later, sirens blasting.

"Quick," he said. "Get me back to the nick – we've got to stop Best." He leapt into the car after throwing his suitcase onto the back seat.

"What hospital is Summer at?" He still wouldn't accept that she could be dying.

"She's critical," Richard replied. "She was flown to Edinburgh this morning."

"Edinburgh! Why there?"

"She needs neurosurgery – it's a specialised unit."

"God," Thomas prayed for her. He yearned to be with her but now she was out of reach.

Richard told Thomas the results of the fingerprint checks.

"Ravir's prints turned up positive. Our friend is a known drugs dealer. He's been deported from New Zealand after doing a stretch for pushing, but we haven't been able to pick him up yet. The Porsche has been found outside Pamela Corran's but not Ravir. We've had her in but she hasn't seen him for two days, says the car wasn't there last night. Thatchit Corran has been down the station too. He's been playing hell, wanting to do Best and Ravir for fraud, theft, criminal damage to his horse – you name it. He was ranting and raving."

"It all fits," Thomas said. "We must get to Sparrow Hawk before its too late. Corran's got nothing to do with this. He's been double-crossed."

Thomas explained his theory in detail to Richard.

"Hell! That's incredible. I'll get on to the airports straight away."

At the station, Thomas sneaked off and tried to telephone Edinburgh, but all he could get from the hospital number was an engaged tone. He slammed the receiver down in anger and joined the others in consultation with the drugs men who were now with senior officers. They, reassuringly, did not look like hippies.

Richard was telephoning the airports at Luton, Gatwick, Cambridge, Stanstead, Heathrow . . . Where would Best come in? Customs at Luton airport had the answer.

"They landed 30 minutes ago and have just left. The party was met by a Frenchman."

Yes, they did have the number of the horsebox.

Richard ran up the stairs with the information. An observation message was passed over the air for all vehicles to apprehend the horsebox, if sighted. On no account was the horse to be left unattended until the arrival of the drugs team.

Thomas telephoned Jed Evans.

"Jed," he said, "good news about the print."

"I heard," Jed said, pleased to hear from him.

"Can I pick your brains?"

"Go ahead," Jed replied.

"How practicable would be the idea of concealing a package inside a horse?"

"What's exactly on your mind Thomas? I mean, how long does this package have to stay inside the horse, and what size package are we talking about?" Thomas decided to put his cards on the table.

"Well, thinking on the lines of the people who have been known to successfully swallow and retain contraceptives containing heroin or cocaine in their stomachs, I want to know what the chances are of a horse being used for the same purpose. Timewise, let's see, we're talking of a flight journey from Paris to England plus a little more."

"That's no problem," Jed said confidently. "Once the packages are in the horse's stomach, then you can safely expect them not to be passed for twenty-four hours. Plenty of time to do that journey."

"What about the unforeseen, such as a grounding due to fog or an airport strike?" Thomas asked.

"Well," Jed considered this, not rushing his answer, "I suppose a smooth-muscle relaxant could be administered such as – Bloody hell, Thomas! You don't think that was what the thief was after, do you?"

"Very much so." Pushing for more information, Thomas pressed on. "How much could you expect to get down a horse?"

Jed again paused before answering. "I suppose the best way to find that out would be to try it but, roughly speaking, I'd say you're probably talking of around thirty-six egg size capsules."

"That's what I was hoping you'd say," Thomas said with enthusiasm. Swiftly calculating loudly enough for Jed to hear, "That's thirty to thirty-six times 200 grams. At the mean average price of £70 a gram that's something between £420,000 and £504,000 worth of coke, a cool half million."

"Well, you know the price of this stuff better than

me," the vet replied. "But as I say, I can't be sure of the exact amounts."

"How could you get these capsules into a horse?"

"Oh, that wouldn't be difficult if you had a quiet co-operative nag."

"Like Sparrow Hawk?" Thomas suggested.

"Ideal," agreed Jed. "You can do what you like to him, a perfect patient. You could either tube him by way of his nostrils or better still you could use a proban or balling gun. Each capsule by this method would have to be resilient and in turn inserted down to the oesophagus, which would then take over, ingesting the capsules into the stomach. All you do then is wait for what comes naturally and recover them at the other end."

"Jed," Thomas asked, "can you get yourself down here now? We might need you." Then, remembering, he added, "I forgot to ask how your mother is."

"That's alright," the vet said. "She's a lot better thanks. I'm expecting her out this weekend. Then my troubles begin! I'll be with you in about ten minutes."

CHAPTER TWENTY

The waiting and hanging around frustrated Thomas and Richard, but the flowing adrenalin wasn't enough to keep Thomas's mind focused on the immediate future. He was finding it hard to concentrate on the outside world. Summer was still with him. The two policemen were in the canteen with the drugs team and Jed Evans who had been briefed. All were drinking coffee and listening to the pocket sets for news of the horsebox.

"Hell, if we don't get them on the road, there's no knowing where they'll take the horse. All we can be sure of is that it won't be going back to Eagle Lodge, and that Ravir is going to cut and run, once he's in receipt of the goods," Richard said agitatedly.

"I'm going to telephone the hospital again," said Thomas and excused himself from the canteen. He tried the number. This time he got through.

"Are you a relative?" he was asked in answer to his enquiry.

"No, a very close friend," he replied.

"Well, her condition is causing a lot of concern. We'll know more after surgery. Phone back tomorrow."

"But . . ."

"I can't tell you any more," the voice interrupted.

"Is there any hope?" he begged.

"She hasn't regained consciousness – I'm sorry. Her parents are at her bedside. Shall I fetch them?"

"No, no thank you," said Thomas, trying to suppress his emotions. "Just tell them I phoned."

He replaced the receiver and returned to the canteen and announced the news before he was asked. The response was a deep silence.

An hour passed and time seemed to be running out, when the telephone rang. A constable in the town had just seen the horsebox taking the roundabout towards the Swindon by-pass. Cars were on the way to intercept.

"At last," the DCI shouted. "Let's go."

The team's excitement grew when they saw the horsebox in the lay-by awaiting their arrival. Best and Ravir were in custody, in the back seats of separate police cars.

"Right," said the Detective Chief Inspector. "Take Mr Evans and make sure that the horse is safe and hasn't deposited the cargo yet. When you search the horsebox make sure Best is with you. Then someone arrange for the horsebox to be taken to the veterinary college for observation. One of you has to stay with it all the time."

CHAPTER TWENTY-ONE

Thomas took the Chief and a DS to Eagle Lodge and showed them around in order that they could familiarise themselves with the scene. Although progress would be delayed until Sparrow Hawk decided otherwise, every other minute of Thomas's time was being taken up by the requirements of PACE. The detention of Best and Ravir had to be substantiated and, with Best especially, they were on thin ice without the solid evidence of the cocaine. Finding time for a coffee break, Thomas picked up a newspaper and read the news that had hit the headlines as predicted.

'*Colic* beats the undefeated champion, Eyecatcher. His condition forces withdrawal from the Arc'.

But the truth behind the headlines was absent. He put the paper down and tried to imagine what tomorrow's headlines would be. He had a good idea – the press would have a field day.

At teatime, Ravir and Best were still in custody and the situation was unlikely to change until the following day. Thomas took the opportunity to visit the people who were looking after Summer's son, Adam. The boy was waiting for him in the lounge, suddenly looking very grown-up. Thomas walked towards him and failed to find words to express his feelings. They understood one another, both sharing the same empty, yearning feeling. They put their hands on each other's shoulders, head to head, and cried.

CHAPTER TWENTY-TWO

At the police station the following day Thomas's thoughts were still with Summer. He had found it more and more difficult to get any news and came to the conclusion that there wasn't any. If the operation had been successful then they weren't raising his hopes – Summer was still in intensive care. But everyone else was on a high; Sparrow Hawk had passed the capsules and they were talking about the biggest drugs coup the force had ever experienced. Jed's estimations had been spot-on.

The Detective Sergeant and Detective Chief Inspector came out of the interview room together with Eric Best, passing Thomas in the corridor on their way to the custody officer. Directing his words to Thomas, the DCI said, "Hang on here, I'll be with you in a minute."

Thomas waited, interested to know what Eric had admitted to and how deeply he had been involved. Five minutes later the DCI returned, alone. "He's coughed! Come into my office and listen to the interview."

Thomas followed the DCI upstairs. "He's asked to make a written statement but insists it has to be to you. I suppose he feels he owes you an explanation, so you'll have to get him out of the cell and start new tapes. Don't look so worried son, you've done them before – not shy are you? Right lad, listen to my interview first and then you'll know what to expect from the statement. We don't want any ambiguities creeping in."

It wasn't that. New legislation under PACE (The Police and Criminal Evidence Act) now required all interviews of defendants who were subject to indictable offences such as manslaughter or drug trafficking to be audio tape-recorded; the procedure was simple and more effective than the laborious taking of contemporaneous notes. He, like every other police officer, had secretly dreaded the day when he'd have to to his first one. There were tight rules and guidelines to cover the chances of anything going wrong but the thought of knowing others would be listening to his voice being played back on a tape, with his mistakes and grammatical errors amplified, had made him cringe. Thomas had by now carried out quite a few such interviews and had become comfortable with the routine, even to the point of enjoying them. This was the first defendant he'd dealt with who had requested to make a written statement after a question and answer interview and didn't pose any problems. However, in normal circumstances, a taped interview would cover everything, making a written statement superfluous. But this was Eric.

Thomas and the Detective Chief Inspector listened for an hour and twenty-eight minutes to the working-tape copies, whilst the DI made notes for a written summary of the transcript.

At the end the Chief Inspector spoke, "OK?

Happy? Go and have a quick cup of tea and do your stuff. He doesn't want his solicitor present so you can carry on whenever you're ready. I've left the exhibits with Sergeant Craig – you might need them."

Thomas had his tea, then went to the custody officer. He explained his purpose, signed Eric out from the cells and was issued with four tapes – C90's to be used in duplicate, one master copy and one working copy. The ruling was that only one side of a tape was ever recorded on, so if the interview were to be extended past forty-five minutes, then a further set of tapes would have to be started.

As they walked to the interview room, Thomas could sense Eric's need to talk.

"Thomas," he said, "I want you to know I'm sorry, truly sorry about Summer. Have you heard how she is? I was only told about the accident two hours ago – that bastard Ravir should swing for it. God, I didn't want this! I said no violence. What have I done!" Eric broke down and started to weep.

Thomas strangely felt a little sympathy for the man. This wasn't going to be easy.

"She's still alive – there's hope, but not much. Look, Eric, please don't say any more until we get into the interview room. Everything has to be recorded these days."

He led Eric into the room and shut the door, switching on the exterior red light which signalled an interview in progress.

Having got back his composure, Eric sat at the table in the seat furthest from the door with Thomas opposite him.

The room, an ex-store cupboard eleven feet by eight feet, was comfortable but smaller than a doctor's consulting room, with walls sound-proofed by soothing pale green acoustic panelling. However, the presence of the sleek, twin-deck, wall-mounted tape recorder next to Thomas dampened any immediate aspirations for intimate conversation. A peep-hole had been newly added in the door to further prevent anyone from walking in and interrupting an interview.

Eric's eyes wandered around the windowless room he hadn't long vacated. The other two empty chairs, the radiator, silent air conditioning and newly carpeted floor, the clock – the Arc would be off in five minutes. There was no telephone. Strange, but Thomas knew he could summon help by the use of a button and that the overhead lamp would inform him of anyone outside wanting to enter. The microphone was on the wall, positioned above the table between them.

"Right," said Thomas, "you want to make a statement. I'll have to record everything, the same as in your interview."

Eric nodded.

"The tape recorder's blind. You have to say 'Yes' in here – nodding is not enough."

"Sorry, I forgot."

Thomas unwrapped two new tapes in front of Eric, like a croupier opening new decks of cards. He placed both into the machine and before switching on to record, explained, "When I start this, there'll be a buzz. This is to indicate the start of the recording. From then on everything said in this room will be recorded. So shall we start?"

Resigned, Eric said, "Yes, I'm ready."

After the buzz, Thomas began as per the guidelines set down in PACE. He said, "This interview is being tape-recorded. I am Police Constable Thomas Cord and I am interviewing Eric Raymond Best. Mr Best, can you please give your full name and date of birth."

Eric obliged.

"Mr Best, could you also confirm that there are no others present at this interview?"

Eric again obliged. Thomas continued by giving the date and time and the fact that the interview was being held at Gordonstow Police Station and added, "At the conclusion of the interview I will give you a notice explaining what will happen to the tapes. You do not have to say anything unless you wish to do so, but what you say may be given in evidence."

"Hold on," Eric interrupted, "do we have to have this recorded? I mean, I'll be signing this statement, won't I?"

With the tape still running, Thomas explained that it would be in Eric's own interest to have the conversation recorded, but Eric still opted to have the tape switched off while he gave his statement.

"As you wish," said Thomas, "but my instructions require that your objections should be recorded on tape. The recording will provide a clear and undisputed account of the interview and it is in your interest that the interview should be recorded. If you still object, please state why."

Eric merely said, "I don't know why. I just don't want it on. There are things I want to say that I don't want taped and I won't get so tongue-tied if it's just you writing."

Thomas then concluded the tape by recording the fact that he was handing Eric the notice as required, followed by the time and date and said, "I am now going to turn the tape off because of the defendant Eric Best's objections."

In the sight of Eric, Thomas stopped the recorder and withdrew both tapes. He marked one as the 'master copy' and the other as the 'working copy'. He signed the sealing label and asked Eric to do the same. Thomas then completed all the relevant details on the label and used it to seal the master tape. He put the two cassettes aside to be handed to the custody officer.

"Right," he said, "shall we get on with it? I understand from what you said earlier that you want me to write your statement down rather than write it yourself." Eric nodded. Thomas wrote down the caution at the head of the statement sheet and asked Eric to sign it.

"I, Eric Raymond Best, wish to make a statement. I want someone to write down what I say. I have been told that I need not say anything unless I wish to do so and that whatever I say will be given in evidence."

Eric signed it using Thomas's pen. "Where shall I start?" he asked Thomas.

"Well, at the beginning's a good place," he replied, slightly humouring Eric to get the tension out of the air. Remembering what Eric had said in the earlier taped interview, he prompted him with, "Tell me of your connection with Ravir."

"I was first introduced to Serge Ravir twelve months ago at a party in Paris thrown to celebrate Eyecatcher's Arc win. It was one of those parties where anything goes and drugs were on the house and being used openly." Eric hesitated, not sure how to continue.

"Do you use drugs?" This gave him the lead.

"I've never used drugs and was appalled to see them being used by people I'd previously considered as respectable, responsible associates. During a quiet moment, when I had been sitting alone, two Frenchmen approached me and asked if I'd consider taking a small package to Britain for them. They were careful not to suggest or mention that it was drugs they were talking about but the fee they had offered for such an insignificant favour left me in no doubt as to what the package would contain."

"Can you remember how much?" asked Thomas.

"No, but it was big money."

"OK, carry on."

"I flatly refused the proposition but, although the men didn't press me further, for a long time after that I was disillusioned by the international racing scene."

"I don't want to spoil your train of thought, but could you slow down a bit?"

"I'm sorry," said Eric, and he continued, carefully trying to keep pace with Thomas's writing.

"Some time last year Thatchit Corran invited me to a promotional dinner for his company. I was to be the guest speaker. I knew nothing about cosmetics but I was able to entertain them with some funny anecdotes about racing. Everything went well, and I must have been very impressionable because I was taken in by the professionalism and style of the entrepreneurs present. Corran, probably sensing my interest in wanting a bit of the action, suggested that I'd be a suitable sleeping partner in a new line he was developing. He asked if I wanted a stake in it. I showed serious interest and things seemed to snowball from then on. The venture was Smudge. All I knew of it initially was that it was a new cosmetic line uniquely directed at the gay market. I considered it as a bit of a risk enterprise myself but Corran presented me with such convincing field researches and figures that I could see that the European market for such an exclusive product was virtually unexplored and that the American potential was astronomical.

"Whether I was the subject of a hard sell and being used as a front man then or whether Corran was being genuine still isn't clear to me. I'd like to think the latter, but all I know is that I wanted in. I could see that Eyecatcher would eventually be going to stud. So the backing of a solid company venture appeared as a wise investment. Anyhow, I went in feet first, and it was a while before I came to learn of the scheming that was going on in France. I suppose I chose not to look under the carpet, so to speak. The money was coming in thick and fast, easy money, and I was looking forward to a time when I could give up training and business altogether and live comfortably on my income. There was so much money coming in, I thought that I'd better put it to some good, and so I applied for planning permission to build a veterinary research centre and stud attached to Eagle Lodge, which would make it the biggest, most complete and best racing establishment in the world. Then the first inkling that something was amiss brought me back to my senses. A note arrived at the stables. It was a clear, pointed threat. A threat to kill Eyecatcher. I was both surprised and frightened. To my knowledge I had done nothing bad to anyone and nothing like this had ever happened to me before. I read the threat over and over. It was in broken English, the postmark and stamp were of French origin. I don't remember it off by heart but the gist of it said something like, 'Settle what you owe for the cultures and Eyecatcher won't be killed'.

"I showed the note to Corran. I wanted to know what the hell was going on, what I was supposed to have owed. I felt this threat an intrusion and told Corran I was informing the police, but Corran coolly took the note and put it into his pocket, saying he would handle it and not to worry. From that, I understood that he knew more about its meaning than I did but I didn't expect him to tell me the truth. So I went to the area in Northern France where the postmark indicated. I can't remember the name of the place now but I have it with the papers in my notebook which was taken from me with the rest of my property when I was arrested. Anyway, I went there to do a bit of research myself and got a first hand account of what had been going on. There was a lot of bitterness and desperation all over, masked with a hope that I was there to honour the contracts which had been drawn up. At first I didn't see why their contracts shouldn't have been honoured. There was plenty of money in the coffers. I was that green. I promised to look into it for them and even settled with one or two of the more demanding growers out of my own pocket there and then.

"When I got home I checked with my solicitors to find out my legal involvement with the company. Unfortunately, I had left it too late. I was told that I was recorded as being the principal British representative of Smudge, and that Corran's name wasn't registered in association with Smudge at all, only the parent company, Eyecatcher. I was out on a limb. I telephoned Corran and told him I wanted out, that I'd pay him the money back even if it meant mortgaging Eagle Lodge but Corran, now knowing that I knew everything, offered me an out only on his terms. I had to listen. I had my back against the wall. Before agreeing to settle with the French farmers and winding up Smudge, Corran wanted to keep it going until after the Arc. He'd already laid his share of the proceeds on Eyecatcher to win again and strongly suggested I should do the same. He said to look on it as a loan and even at this stage he sounded credible. He said that after Eyecatcher's win there'd be enough money to buy off the culture growers and plenty over to allow me to keep what I'd already received from the venture. But the only flaw in Corran's theory was Eyecatcher himself. I knew that his *colic* would prevent him from winning another Arc and that the only time to bet on him would be on the day of the race when I'd know that he was fully fit, unaffected by *colic* and at the starting post ready to do himself justice.

"Corran, though, had already backed him ante-post to ensure he'd got the best possible price available, but this meant if Eyecatcher didn't run he'd lose all his stake. Eyecatcher by this time was from what I recall 4/1 on for the Arc, unbackable odds for my stake, so I thought, sod you, I'd play along but protect my own interests. I didn't like the sneaky bastard before, but now I hated him – he had trapped me. The more I thought about Eyecatcher, the more convinced I was that he wouldn't win. Great though he was, experience had told me he hated travelling abroad and the *colic* of the first French trip would stay in his memory until he got back on that plane. Whatever the cause, his fears would return and so would his *colic,* only this time it would be more severe. No, I definitely couldn't see him winning again. I was desperate. I racked my brains for another way out and decided that there was no other alternative but to go to the police. Then, just as I had lost all hope, I got this phone call out of the blue from Ravir. He reintroduced himself and asked if I had given any further thought to the favour he was asking. He said his auntie was still waiting for the parcel but she could wait until the next Arc. I instinctively knew that this was drugs again but agreed to meet him on my terms. I didn't want to be used again. I didn't want to be made a scapegoat, a decoy for a bigger consignment. So I used my veterinary education to work out how much I could safely smuggle inside a horse and when I arrived at an amount, I insisted upon moving that quantity or nothing.

"I told Ravir the plan but he couldn't give an answer at once. I suppose he had to have top level clearance, but he contacted me the following day with the OK. Ravir insisted on supervising the operation. He or his bosses didn't trust me, but it left me with a problem. I didn't know how to explain his presence to the satisfaction of Corran and the stable staff. So I was quite pleased with myself when I came up with the brainwave of having Ravir pose as a stable lad – something he didn't take kindly to, but it fitted in well with past events. There was still the underlying possibility of some bitter or impatient culture-producer carrying out some sort of vengeful attack on Eyecatcher and the cameras would, in turn, keep Corran satisfied as to the need for Ravir. Now as far as the drugs smuggling was concerned, realistically I didn't want to put my trust in Eyecatcher. It would have been no good at all if he were to have an attack of *colic* while he was stuffed with the cargo and I felt no qualms about cutting Corran out of his chance to land his bet, after the way he'd stitched me up. So it was left to me to find a ringer, a double of Eyecatcher. However, I knew that the horse wasn't going to race and therefore wasn't going to be checked by French racing authorities or vets, provided I withdrew him in time, so I searched and found a horse that would fit the bill – Sparrow Hawk.

"He was an ideal swop, perfectly level headed, a cool calm traveller with a soft nature. He couldn't care less what you did to him and the old fashioned balling gun being put down his throat didn't worry him in the least. I had left nothing to chance and we even carried out an experimental trial, inserting what was to be the egg-sized containers into him to be satisfied that they'd be retained for sufficent time. That, by the way, was the real reason why you were stopped from coming around to sculpt Eyecatcher. We didn't want you being there when a container was passed in the droppings, did we? On the occasion that you came when Ravir was there it was actually Sparrow Hawk and not Eyecatcher in the box but Ravir left the rugs on deliberately so you wouldn't see the difference. Besides, Ravir didn't feel comfortable with a policeman around. So, I'm afraid Corran had nothing to do with stopping you carrying on with your sculpture. In fact, I still don't think he knows anything about it."

"You don't want me to put that down, do you?" interrupted Thomas, not wanting the fact that he was sculpting one of the horses involved in the crime to be introduced into the statement.

"No," said Eric, "I just thought I'd mention it for your benefit." He read the last few words he had said before that and continued from 'for sufficient time'.

"But Ravir didn't have my confidence in a horse's digestive system. He wanted to have the added insurance of using something that would ensure that Sparrow Hawk didn't pass the stuff prematurely. I told him the only things which could be used were a few commercial stomach relaxants that I'd mentioned, because if they were found in our possession during transit to Paris, then they could be accounted for with Eyecatcher being *colic* prone. But I couldn't get legal access to these drugs without directly asking a vet for them, something I didn't want to do, as a vet would insist on administering it himself. I told Ravir not to worry and that we were guaranteed twenty-four hours but, needless to say, Ravir didn't accept that and must have done that awful burglary on Jed's place. I knew it when he handed me the Buscopan the following day. I'd already heard the news of the fire but what could I do except lose my temper? The damage had been done by then and this man didn't mess about. As I said, the burglary and fire were unnecessary and awful and I'm sorry it happened. I didn't have to use any of the stuff, there was no need. I'm relieved to hear Mrs Evans isn't too bad.

"As it was never the intention to race Sparrow Hawk or Eyecatcher in the Arc, the passport wasn't going to be seen by the French stewards, but I had to do enough to deceive the customs or anyone else likely to do a check. A doctored, dry powder copy of the descriptive form, suitably embossed and substituted for the real one, was all that was needed. In fact, it would be totally possible to race with a ringer for that matter, the forgery is that easy. I mean, after altering the description to suit and swopping it in the passport, it was only left for me to get the paper embossed. To do this, I just had to go to a printing supplier and have a stamp made up. It cost me £22, that's all, without any questions. I then swopped Eyecatcher and Sparrow Hawk around and took Sparrow Hawk to France as Eyecatcher, while Eyecatcher himself was moved from Eagle Lodge, but left in England."

"To me, you still sound enthusiastic about all this," Thomas commented.

"I'm not – it's just that it was so easy and I reckon it could still be done successfully."

Thomas interrupted. "Eric, there's a point I'm not clear about. You told Summer that Sparrow Hawk was schooling for the jumps. Is this right?"

Eric answered, "That's what I wanted her to believe, yes, but Sparrow Hawk was in France with me and Eyecatcher remained anonymously in a field. He wasn't actually being schooled as Sparrow Hawk at all. That was just something I made up to stop Summer from questioning the absence of Sparrow Hawk; after all, I wouldn't leave him at Eagle Lodge as Summer knew them so well – she'd see the switch. Now are you with me?" he asked Thomas.

"Yes, it's important to have it fully explained in the statement, that's all."

"I see, but I was coming to it. Shall I carry on?"

Thomas nodded, and Eric continued, hoping to clear up any ambiguity for him.

"In Chantily I was met by the other man who had been with Ravir the first time we'd met in the Paris party. I don't know his name. He gave me the packages to be put in Sparrow Hawk already prepared. Ravir had stayed in England to arrange the hiding of Eyecatcher until I returned with Sparrow Hawk. I'd told Summer that Sparrow Hawk would be away schooling for the jumps for a few days and I'd arrange his return. Of course, this was Eyecatcher. The intention was to return him to Eagle Lodge when Summer was occupied elsewhere. I'd entered a runner up in Scotland which should have kept her out of the way for long enough. I wasn't to know the heavy rain there would lead to the cancellation of the meeting and the tragic accident."

Eric reached across the table to offer his hand in condolence or to touch Thomas's hand in reassurance. Thomas wasn't sure which. He withdrew his hand before contact was made saying, "Let's keep this formal please, Eric."

"Of course," Eric returned, "but I just . . ." He didn't finish attempting to justify himself, instead he continued his statement. He read the last line upside down to recall where he'd got to.

"Before this happened to Summer I withdrew Eyecatcher, who was in fact Sparrow Hawk, from the race. I had previously announced to the racing authorities that the horse had developed a *colic* condition which I was hoping I could clear successfully enough for him to race, but I subsequently reported that although he was over the condition he had been weakened too much to do himself justice and would not recover in time for the Arc. Then, once examined and declared fit to travel back to England, I was free to put the drugs into his stomach and fly him back. It seemed so easy, I can't see why no one's ever done it before. I waited at Luton to be collected by Ravir, the air transport people having left me. I knew nothing of Summer being knocked down. In fact, I didn't even know that Hamilton had been rained off. When he arrived, Ravir said there was a change of plan. We wouldn't be taking Sparrow Hawk, who was now still holding the cocaine, back to Eagle Lodge until the drugs had been recovered. I asked him why and he said less risk. The rest I think you know. I don't know where we would have gone to with Sparrow Hawk to recover the drugs. Ravir, I think now, was just driving, looking for an isolated lay-by or somewhere until the horse had passed them and then he probably would have left me to carry the can. Anyway, it didn't come to that because you lot turned up."

Thomas sat back and said, "Is that it?"

"Yes," answered Eric, as if relieved to get if off his chest.

"Right then," said Thomas. "Read it, add or alter anything you want and then sign it here, here and at the end of each page." He indicated to Eric where he was required to sign the statement. "You'll notice that I haven't left any paragraph spaces. That's not bad punctuating, it's done to stop extra words you didn't say being added to your statement." Eric didn't bother to read it so Thomas passed him a card on which a paragraph was printed.

"Right," he said, "if you're satisfied, write this after it."

Eric read the words on the card and copied them down at the conclusion of his statement:

"I have read the above statement and I have been told that I can correct, alter, or add anything I wish. This statement is true, and I have made it of my own free will." He signed this also.

Thomas rose, collected the statement sheets and tapped them until they were neatly together and picked up the tapes. "What do you think will happen now?" Eric asked him.

Thomas looked at him seriously, and said, "I honestly don't know. You'll be charged for the offences under the Missuse of Drugs Act. Probably only the importing of a controlled drug as a holding charge, and then I don't know – it depends. All I can tell you is that I can see you going down for a long stretch."

"Will I have bail?" Eric inquired, half panicking, half pleading. "I've got to sort things out at the stables."

"It's possible, but it's not up to me," answered Thomas. "It depends on your solicitor. If you can get a big enough surety and surrender your passport, then maybe. You'll have to talk to him."

"Well, I'd like to sort things out before I wind the yard up. You know, return the horses to their owners, say goodbye to the staff." He was close to tears again and looked ashen white. It was now getting home to him that he had lost everything. There would be no need for the Jockey Club to tell him that his licence would be taken away – he had already realised that. Thomas could see a broken man. He hoped that if he was to get bail, he wouldn't use the opportunity to take his own life.

Not knowing quite what to say, Thomas just offered, "I suppose the only one with something to look forward to out of all this is Eyecatcher. He'll be returned to his owners for stud duties. Sparrow Hawk will be treated like a king too – at least until the case is over and then it will be up to the court to decide his fate. I should expect him to be offered up at auction to race again, under new ownership. He looked at Eric with an expression which summed up his feelings of unwarranted waste. "Thank you for being so honest with me. Your openness will undoubtedly help us to prove the case against Ravir but, nice as it will feel to nail him, I needn't say that I'm sorry it was you." Thomas held open the interview room door for Eric and together they walked into the corridor, Thomas keeping close as he escorted him back to the cells. Two PC's came downstairs from the canteen. As they passed him, one said, "Dummy!"

"Ff . . . oh, why don't you piss off!" shouted back Thomas.

They walked on laughing.

"What was all that about?" asked Eric.

"Oh, nothing. I've just been caught for another quid that's all." He handed Eric and the tapes over to the Custody Officer and went upstairs to the canteen.

"Well? Good statement?" asked the DCI.

"More of an epic than a statement," Thomas answered, handing him the sheets to read, "but it's all there." He flexed his hand to relieve the cramp that was setting in from all the writing.

"Good. Better to have too much than too little. If

Best's solicitor had had his way, he wouldn't have cooperated with us at all. Do you know, that stubborn bastard Ravir has said eff all? A fat lot of good it'll do him though. We've got him on arson and attempted murder of Mrs Evans. Hopefully, we'll get him for your girlfriend as well, but if she doesn't pull through we're struggling to prove manslaughter."

Thomas slumped into a chair, "I'm knackered. OK if I finish, Sir? I feel like I'm in a goldfish bowl, everything's going on around me but I don't feel part of it."

"Yeh, go ahead, I'll get one of the others to fingerprint Best, but stay handy in case we want to get hold of you at short notice. When are you on next?"

Thomas let out a sigh, "I don't know now, I'll have to check the duty roster."

The Chief Inspector didn't hear the reply, already too engrossed with the statement. "This bit about planning to do it again and the emboss stamp, perhaps we should advise Weatherby's to revise their system and of course the customs will be interested in this new way to bring drugs in. Well, off you go then."

Thomas entered up his pocket book and with nothing more left for him to do, went home. His statement, which he'd only have to copy from his book, would consist mainly of events after the arrest as most of what had happened previously was only hearsay and could be concentrated into the convenient term, 'As a result of information received'.

Thomas reflected on the statement that Eric had given and the short discussion which had followed.

He was relieved that Eric hadn't asked what would be done about Corran's exploits. The fact still remained that Corran hadn't done enough to be pulled in let alone charged. Perhaps the Fraud Squad would compile a file for the DPP but he'd been very cunning and Thomas had to accept the fact that he was going to get away with it, only having to suffer the loss of his massive stake forfeited by the withdrawal of Eyecatcher from the Arc. Eric wouldn't be happy to learn of Corran getting off so lightly.

CHAPTER TWENTY-THREE

"Thomas!" Richard called as he ran after him outside the station. Thomas turned and waited for his friend to catch up.

"Hang on, I'll give you a lift home. How are you feeling?" The answer was so obvious, Richard felt a bit stupid for asking, but the words had left his lips before he'd had a chance to rephrase them. Thomas wanted to say he felt lonely but instead answered, "I wish it was all over. Ravir's not going to cop it, is he? What do you think happened?"

Richard knew he was referring to Summer's accident. "The same as you. Ravir came back to the stable late to return Eyecatcher, but Summer disturbed him. He probably tried to shut her up and chased after her as she tried to get away on the horse . . . and then the accident."

"Yeh, that's what I make of it," said Thomas. "As the DCI said, without a confession or Summer's evidence we're struggling to prove it. A clever lawyer is going to turn it on its head, probably claim Eyecatcher bolted, and when Ravir gave chase to try and save Summer, the lorry knocked her down. Ravir will say he panicked and drove off. All very plausible to a jury – and the attempted murder of Mrs Evans is no stronger – if Ravir denies making that phonecall, he can claim that he was of the opinion that the house was empty and, with her being deaf, it's again plausible."

Richard had to agree, the only concrete evidence they had against Ravir merely proved the burglary and arson. "Listen," he said, as they got into the police car. "I think you ought to know that if the worst comes to the worst and Summer dies the drugs squad are talking about a deal. Ravir's indicated that he can put them onto the main man, if we drop the attempted murder charge."

"That's all very well," said Thomas angrily, "but what happens if Summer dies and there's an inquest? Accidental death or a finding of death by misadventure I suppose. How is Adam going to accept that? I couldn't tell him we did a deal with his mother's killer."

"But we don't know, Thomas. If she dies, we still won't know if he intended killing her."

"Of course he fucking did!"

Richard could see he'd have to choose his words more carefully. "Sorry, all right then, what I meant was, we know he did it, but we might not be able to prove it. Look, don't think it's my idea to do a deal. I'm only telling you what's going on behind the scenes. I can see your point, I can see their point. If the drugs boys can get more out of it, why not, they're only after a result too, and if for some reason Ravir fails to do the business, he still gets done for drug smuggling which will hit him as hard as the attempted murder charge would."

Thomas saw the logic. "OK," he said, "tell them to go ahead, but don't involve me."

"Don't worry," replied Richard sympathetically, "we're all on the same side."

With everything more or less settled, Richard dropped Thomas at his home and left. Thomas still had holidays owing to him, with evenings for him and Richard to get drunk, but he had Summer to worry about. He'd planned to drive up to Scotland the following day, to be at her bedside, already resigned to the fact that he would never be able to do the long journey before having a night's sleep. He wondered how he could tell Adam the result of the inquiry. Probably by telling the truth, but it wouldn't be easy. He thought of taking him to a football match, something special. It would be an opportunity for them to get closer before he explained how the police were not infallible and how they had failed to prove that Summer's death, if it came to that, was not an accident. He promised himself to phone Adam first thing in the morning. And there was the sculpture. One of his days would have to be put aside to get it mounted and delivered to Pamela, but he didn't want to see her again and hoped he'd be able to leave it at the salon for her when she was out.

* * *

The following morning Thomas was blasted into consciousness by his alarm clock. He hadn't heard it for so long that when it went off, he didn't know what it was, where he was, or what day it was. Startled, he jumped up in bed and looked to the side for his boots. One was missing. He frantically moved his clothes searching for it, before realising he was at home and this was his day off.

Reality flooded back. If only it had been a bad dream. He turned and saw his wife drawing back the curtains on a bright new day. She looked at him with maternal eyes. He recognised a change. She had a glow of contentment about her, happy for the first time in a long time. She walked over and sat on the bed beside him, kissing his forehead. Slowly, gently, she offered her hand, unsure of his response. She searched for forgiveness. Thomas, unable to share his grief with her, took her hand and put his arm around her. The telephone rang.

"I'll get it." Cathy stood up and went downstairs to answer it.

"It's for you. It's the hospital," she shouted up to Thomas.

He rushed down and she handed him the receiver. He took it from her and as she went to make the breakfast, he dreaded what he was going to hear and steeled himself before saying, "Thomas Cord."

As the voice at the other end spoke, Thomas felt his smile rise like the morning sun, until his face was beaming. He was unable to hold back his happiness as it burst into joy.

A little boy ran past him from upstairs, wearing his other boot. He looked up at Thomas.

"Hello, my name's Stuart. What's your name?"

"Doorstop," he said as he laughed.